THE POSSUM HUNTER

by

S. EARL WILSON, III

PublishAmerica
Baltimore

© 2008 by S. Earl Wilson, III.
All rights reserved. No part of this book may be reproduced, stored in a retrieval system or transmitted in any form or by any means without the prior written permission of the publishers, except by a reviewer who may quote brief passages in a review to be printed in a newspaper, magazine or journal.

First printing

PublishAmerica has allowed this work to remain exactly as the author intended, verbatim, without editorial input.

All characters in this book are fictitious, and any resemblance to real persons, living or dead, is coincidental.

ISBN: 1-60672-293-X (softcover)
ISBN: 978-1-4489-1119-6 (hardcover)
PUBLISHED BY PUBLISHAMERICA, LLLP
www.publishamerica.com
Baltimore

Printed in the United States of America

This book is dedicated to Brenda Tisdale Smith and Anita "Vickie" Smith, without whom it would not have been possible to complete.
Thank you both!

With special thanks to Mr. Earl Burkett, Mr. Howard Brown, Mr. Isiah Easterling and Mr. Thomas Earl Toney.

Illustrations by Michael Wheaton

INTRODUCTION

"Possum up the simmon tree,
Raccoon on the ground.
Said the raccoon to the possum,
"Throw some simmons down, boy
Throw some simmons down.
Throw some simmons down, boy
Throw some simmons down."

We used to sing this when I was a boy living in the Springfield community, Route 5, Hattiesburg, Mississippi. Needless to say, I was a country boy who lived in the country and listened to country music on the radio. It didn't matter that I was Negroid and worshipped white country singers. It was something to do when there was nothing else to do.

If you were a country boy and your parents were schoolteachers, not farmers, you always needed something to do to rid your mind of boredomness. The children my age were always busy from "sun up" till "sun down" with chores on their parents' farms, like plowing, planting, chopping, harvesting, milking the cows, churning the butter, leading the cows to the pasture and bringing them back in the evenings. "I envy them," I thought. They could ride mules and sleighs, pick cotton, peas, beans, corn, tomatoes, cucumbers, etc. and sing while doing so. My readings, which I was required to do, often mentioned Negroes singing while working, even back home in Africa. They all seemed to be having so much fun while I was stuck at home reading *Tom Sawyer*,

S. EARL WILSON, III

Huckleberry Finn, or *The Last of the Mohicans* and singing and pumping water from the well.

When my parents gave me the liberty to work with my friends in the fields, I suddenly discovered how wrong I was and why most of the kids, after reaching the ripe old ages of seventeen or eighteen, deserted their family's farms and never returned. They found jobs in town (Hattiesburg), Detroit, Chicago, Los Angeles, Joliet, Gary or anywhere far away from the country and farms. I can hardly recall any of them returning to reclaim the acres of land bequeathed to them by their parents, resuming their former occupations, and turning it into luxurious, profitable farms or dairy lands.

Some were lucky and fortunate enough that when the cities' boundaries were extended to encase their land and subdivision homes were being built to accommodate the expansion, they got good money, thousands of dollars for selling their land. A few others, who had financially successful lives and good retirement income, returned and built beautiful homes on their old estates. They may have had gardens but never farms. One such person, now a preacher, said that he had toiled so hard to raise and gather peas and beans that he would never sow or reap them again as long as supermarkets sold them.

THE POSSUM HUNTER

Being an ex "town boy" (Hattiesburg is really a city but then we referred to it then as a "town"), the town people referred to us as "country," not suburban, as today, I began quickly to adopt country ways. Eating country food, hunting, fishing, gardening, and raising chickens and hogs all became a part of my life's rituals. Having sex with girls was also a part of country traditions, but this somehow evaded me like a kitten running from a dog or a mouse avoiding a cat. Other than sex, I became a bonafide, metamorphosized country boy with my father's Buicks to drive instead of a pickup truck or a mule and wagon.

The hunting aspect of my life introduced me to squirrels, rabbits, birds, coons, and possums. Hunting events always included tall tale tellings, and we were all avid listeners, especially when old adults told their stories, truth or fiction. This is how I got to know about Roscoe Mordecai Johnson's life.

What do opossums and raccoons have in common? Plenty—they both belong to phylum chordate, class mammalian; they both have feet that resemble human hands with thumbs; they both basically are nocturnal animals who stir and eat at night. Their diets are similar in that they both are omnivorous, meaning they eat both plants and animals. Opossums are not very finicky. They eat cockroaches, beetles, mosquitoes, dead animals, frogs, fruit, berries, birds and their eggs, corn, snails and earthworms. The raccoon's diet includes frogs, fruit, nuts, berries, rodents, eggs, crayfish, and corn.

All of these things, Roscoe Mordecai Johnson knew well as he hunted them, not for pets or for their furs, but for food for the poorer echelon in Hungerville, Mississippi—sometimes for the elite also. Their status of middle or upper class did not deny them the pleasure of tasting roasted opossum or coon in gravy/sauce with roasted apples and potatoes, along with collard greens and cornbread.

The highfaluting Negroes could cook their own possums or sometimes hire a country girl to whip up a meal for them and promise not to tell anyone. The well-to-do white people already had colored folks in their kitchens who knew better than to tell. But they told anyway—to other blacks and poor whites. "Honey chile, you know I cooked up some possum and sweet potatoes for the Allison family yesterday. Mr. and Mrs. Allison ate it like it was their last meal. All the children, except for Thomas Jr., turned their heads and refused to partake in such a 'primitive festival.' At the urging of their father, who threatened to cut off their allowances, they ate a little bit and declared the meal 'disgusting.' For them I fried some chicken."

Mordecai's first encounter with an opossum was purely accidental. He was as hungry as hell, gathering lida knots for kindling for his mother to prepare whatever they would have to eat tonight. It was Wednesday and he, his mother Rebecca, his father Oscar, and little sister Rose hadn't had any meat to eat since Sunday when they fried their next to last chicken, feet included. Couldn't afford to ring the neck of the only chicken left; they had to have eggs to eat. He had taken with him a croaker sack and his .22 rifle to shoot a rabbit or a squirrel, if he was lucky enough to see one. Mordecai's luck was bad. He didn't see anything to shoot at. He was startled with the sudden appearance of a creature that he had never before seen. It was extremely ugly with a tail without any hair, ears without hair, a tapered head with a pointed muzzle, pink nose, glittering black eyes, feet with pink toes, a dense woolly gray fur, and a white face.

The opossum started to run or waddle away from Mordecai. Mordecai yelled, aimed his rifle, and shot at him. He missed, but the possum fell over like he was dead, his eyes closed and his tongue extended out of his mouth. He was simply "playing possum." That didn't make no never mind to Mordecai. He picked the possum up by his scaly tail and put him in his croaker sack.

THE POSSUM HUNTER

When he took him home, Rebecca, his mother, rejoiced after seeing what they had and shot the possum again, this time in the head, just to make sure. There would be plenty of meat tonight and the following two days. She had her husband Oscar take the lida knots and build a fire to heat the water to scale the possum of his fur. "No," said Oscar, "let's skin him and keep the fur." This they did and used the hot water to boil the possum, with salt and pepper added, before baking him in the oven.

That night at supper, a smile spread from the cheeks of Mordecai as his mother placed the well seasoned possum, along with sweet potatoes and collard greens, before the family. His apprehension faded with each bite. It was as good as rabbit, squirrel, and chicken and better than pork chops. They all ate well.

Mordecai was all of eight years old when he first encountered the opossum and began to listen and learn from others about their habitats and ways. He thought that there was no adventure greater than possum hunting, and he became an avid hunter not only for his family but for other people as well. He found that he could sell opossums to both blacks and whites, rich or poor. He would charge the more affluent people more money, and they didn't "winch" at the price. Sometimes the poor people would try to barter by offering him potatoes, corn, okra, eggs, milk, or watermelons. Sometimes he accepted.

Once, he accepted a puppy as a trade. He was a coon dog, and Mordecai named him "Buck." Buck brought much joy into the lives of the Johnson family. Everybody was happy with Buck just as he was, until big meeting day at East Pine Methodist Church in Springfield. Mordecai, now 13 years old, had brought his puppy and tied him by rope to a shade tree, where he sat peacefully and eating any food that was brought to him.

When Lonzo Brown saw the dog tied to a tree, he jokingly asked, "Whose mutt is this and how come he is tied up?"

Mordecai got "hot under the collar" and began to defend his dog's honor. "He ain't no mutt. He a coon dog that the Tatums gave to me for a possum."

Well, how come he tied up?"

"So he won't run away and get lost."

Lonzo said, "Real coon dogs don't run away and they never get lost. If they do, they will always go back home."

"You shore?" Mordecai asked.

"Loose him and see," Lonzo said.

Mordecai untied Buck while the crowd of church people watched to see the reaction. Buck did nothing except move closer towards Mordecai's side. He was loyal and did not run away.

"Well, that shows that he is loyal to you but what would happen if all of you and your folks was to go back into the church and leave him alone?"

This they reluctantly did and stayed for the next sermon. After the hour and a half sermon was over, they went back outside. Buck was still there waiting patiently by the shade tree for their return. They were all happy and proud.

"Well, I guess he got the loyalty of a coon dog, but how many coons had he found?"

"None," said Mordecai, "and I ain't never seen a coon."

"It's hard to see em ifen you ain't looking for them or don't hunt for them and that has to be at night time. They is night animals that taste sweeter than possum and chicken. Bring him over to my house tomorrow night about seven, and we will hook him up with my coon dogs "Blue" and "Florida" and go coon hunting. He'll learn how to be what he's susposed to be."

Mordecai and Buck arrived at Lonzo's house about 6:30 p.m the next day, early enough to help Alonzo's mother and father, his younger sister, his two older brothers, and two older sisters finish eating their supper of raccoon and Irish potatoes. For something that he had never seen, it tasted pretty good.

After the meal, Lonzo took Mordecai and Buck to the backyard and showed them a real live raccoon enclosed in a bin. Buck began to bark at the creature. "A good sign," Lonzo said.

What Mordecai saw was something that resembled both a cat and a dog and weighed around 14 pounds. Its fur was a grizzled gray color with silver tips. It had a broad head, pointed nose and black eyes. Its ears stood straight up and were about an inch long. Unlike the possum's scaly

THE POSSUM HUNTER

tail, it had a bushy tail with four brown rings around it. The face was a black mask outlined in white. Not too ugly but strange indeed if you were seeing it for the first time.

Lonzo told Mordecai a little bit about the animal they were going to hunt. "It often lives in hollow trees and logs and sometimes uses the ground burrows of other animals for raising their young or for sleeping during the coldest part of winter months. Winter is the raccoon's greatest enemy because their food is scarcer then."

"They seem to like to be near or in the vicinity of stream edges, open forest, and coastal marshes. Their tracks are easy to follow because they are paired, having one rear foot beside one front one. The raccoon has five toes and usually the claw marks are seen in the mud or ground. The back foot makes a print which the toes and heel pad are joined. The front track's toe and heel pad have a small space between, making them look like a pair of small human hands."

Let the game begin! They were off and running round around 7:35 p.m. Darkness was approaching. All of them, Mordecai, Lonzo, his two brothers Jim and Johnnie B., and the youngest of the three sisters Fannie Mae, who wore britches and brogans like the males and a skull cap on her head to protect her hair from the briars and bushes. She really looked different than she did at the dining room table with her hair slightly long and greasy with pomade and ribbons in it, her pretty legs shining with Vaseline on them, and one of the prettiest faces that Mordecai had ever seen. He had always admired her at Sunday school and high school but was too scared to say anything to her. Fannie Mae sensed Mordecai's affection for her but did nothing to encourage him. The first move would have to come from him. She was giving him a chance to do so by accompanying them on this trip.

The dogs, Florida and Blue, both took a liking to Buck and he to them. A good omen, they all thought. They put reins on all three and took them deeper into the woods. Fannie Mae, breaking the silence between them, asked Mordecai if she could handle Buck. He readily agreed and spoke to her for the very first time, "You sure you want to, honey?"

"Yeah, I want to, but why you call me honey?"

Mordecai, grinning and sweating and nervous as hell, said, "Cause I think you is as sweet as honey."

"Does that mean you love me, baby?"

Before he could answer her, Lonzo butted in. "Fannie Mae, quit your flirting wit Mordecai now. Do it after the hunting. His mind need to be on coons now, not on pussy! We all know you been liking him for a long time."

"Oh, Lonzo, shut up. You make me feel shamed."

"Please don't be shamed, Fannie Mae," said Mordecai. "Is it true that you really like me?"

"Yes," she said.

"Well, I'm proud as hell cause I love you, too." He couldn't believe he said this. Thus, love begins on a coon hunt.

They took the dogs down by the branch creek and turned them loose. They all tried to follow as fast as they could through briars, water, tree limbs, uphill, downhill, bushes, and swamps.

You would have to be in pretty good physical condition to do this and to keep up. To Mordecai's surprise, Buck left him and Fannie Mae kept the pace as well as the others. Her sex was no hindrance. She would make some man a very good wife, thought Mordecai. Perhaps himself—they could hunt together.

When the dogs began to howl and bark profusely, they knew that a coon had been found and treed. The hunting party ran like they were in the Olympics. When they stopped, they saw the glittering eyes of the coon behind a white mask up a cedar tree. Someone had to climb the tree and shake him down. That was Johnnie B's job. He scaled the tree with the ease of a squirrel and violently shook the limb that the coon had attached himself to. The coon fell and hit the ground with a thud. The dogs surrounded him, denying him escape as the coon prepared to fight. His teeth could harm the dogs and any man's hand that was foolish enough to try and handle him. Thus, Lonzo shot him through his head with his .22 rifle. Unlike possums, the raccoon is rarely taken home alive. He can cause a great deal of damage to the hunter or to his dogs. He is, perhaps, more profitable than the opossum. Some are as big as the dogs that pursue them and their furs can be used or sold for clothing.

THE POSSUM HUNTER

The night was profitable. It yielded two coons as big as dogs and three large opossums. Mordecai and Fannie Mae held left hands while they both carried a croaker sack with an opossum in it with their right hands. Lonz and Jim toted the dead coons and a possum.

It was about midnight when Mordecai left Lonzo's house with his coon and a possum, both prepared for cooking. He learned how to nail a coon to a tree and skin him, plus how to rid him of his internal organs (guts). He learned something new about preparing possums, too. Instead of using hot water and scaling them of their hair with a blade, they placed them into their fireplace, fueled with hot burning wood/coal embers and burnt the hair off. To be certain that the hair was all gone the meat would become almost black in color from the singeing. The possum would then be washed and cleaned to remove anything remaining, then boiled before being cooked in the oven.

He took with him home a cleaned and almost boiled possum, a naked, dressed coon that Fannie Mae had prepared for him, all wrapped in flour sacks. All his mother had to do was season them with salt and pepper, bacon grease and garlic and onion and rubbed with lard, then bake them in the oven. Is this an epicurean delight or not? Mordecai placed his bounty, himself and Buck on the "ground slide" pulled by his mule Josh and headed home.

Before he left, Fannie Mae pulled him around to the back of the house and placed her lips upon his lips. She pulled off her skull cap and let her hair fall. She then stepped out of her britches, pulled off her shirt, and stood naked before him, wearing only her brogan shoes. Mordecai ran his hands all over her more softer than cotton body. Who knows just what would have happened had they not heard somebody coming. Fannie grabbed her clothing and ran behind the chicken coop to hide. Mordecai couldn't run, so he pretended he was peeing.

"Oh, excuse me," said the other sister, Mae Helen. "I was looking for some more kindling for the stove to finish cooking. Will you help me take some in?" she asked.

"I shore will," he said as he gathered some wood and lida knots.

"Giddy up, Josh." The ground slide slid effortlessly over the grass and headed home with its passengers and bounty.

That next Sunday at church, Mordecai and Fannie Mae met again. This time they did not pretend not to notice each other but came together without reservation. There was now a bond between them. The coon hunting episode wiped out any apprehensions and they came together like old friends.

"I missed you, Fannie Mae," he said. "What you been doing?"

"Thinking about you every night, wishing that you wuz in bed with me," Fannie said.

"Shore nuff?" Mordecai asked with excitement in his voice.

"Shore nuff!" she answered.

There were no movies to go to or drugstores with ice cream parlors with sundaes, malts, and shakes or amusement parks or places for teenagers to go and mingle. This was the country.

"What are we going to do?" he asked.

"My mamma and popper already know that we like each other and they both tease me about you. You could come over to my house this evening after church, have dinner with us, play some checkers, then maybe we could take a ride on your ground slide," she said. (A ground slide is a wooden contraption made of wood with bottom rails made of tough oak, smoothed by sanding and then shaped like a bow. A deck is built on top of them for riding and carrying loads. These loads could be people, logs, equipment, coon, possums, or anything. It is usually pulled by mules or horses or oxen. In this case, it was mule.)

Mordecai rode his ground slide to Fannie Mae's house round about 6:30 p.m. His belly was full, and he didn't eat because Rebecca, his mother, insisted that he eat Sunday dinner at home instead of going to other folks' house to eat, making his family look bad. Besides that, they had fried two chickens that his daddy had traded a possum for. He did eat some sweet potato pie that Fannie swore she had baked.

Lonzo and them all, except his mother, went outside to play with the coon that they had adopted. This left Fannie Mae and Mordecai alone together in the so-called living room. They played checkers and kissed softly. Fannie was getting hot, so she opened up her blouse. She didn't wear a "brar," so her bare breast was showing. She moved to Mordecai and placed her tits in his mouth. Instinctly, he began to suck them. This aroused her even more. She then unzipped his pants and took out his already hard penis. Mordecai wanted to shout but she placed her finger to her lips and said, "Shhee," meaning don't make a sound. She then turned her back to him, sat across his knees, lifted her dress, and sat down on him as his penis entered her vagina. They both almost lost control and moaned very loud. Fannie began her up and down movements while Mordecai tried to follow. Their rhythm was off only momentarily, then it was symmetrical. If they thought someone was coming, Fannie would simply stop and jump up and move away while Mordecai covered his penis with his cap. If no one came, they resumed their lovemaking until the climax, where she jumped up in order not to get pregnant. She helped him finish by using a piece of cloth and her hands.

Mordecai was thrilled to the utmost. He had masturbated several times before but that didn't compare to real pussy and a female's helping hand. He had lost his virginity. Evidently, this was not the first time for Fannie. She had done it twice before, once with the preacher's son that she courted last year and also with the city boy who walked her home after the revival. There was no need for them to hide then. They were already walking in the woods, so he just spread his jacket on the ground for her to lay upon.

Both times were good, but they just didn't compare with the excitement and thrill she just had now with Mordecai. Besides, she didn't love either of them anyways, but she was stone in love with Mordecai. "I'm going to marry this colored boy," she told herself.

They became almost inseparable. Anywhere she went at school he was there, except when she had to go to the toilet. Everybody knew that Fannie was Mordecai's girlfriend and he was her man. Didn't do nobody no good to try to "go with" either one of them because it was impossible to break their love for each other up. Pepper Smith tried to get next to Fannie Mae by writing her love notes and slipping them to her with pieces of candy in them. Once, he placed two bits in his note. Fannie Mae told him no and she showed the notes to Mordecai. Mordecai took the quarter, punched Pepper in the belly, and threw the two bit piece at his feet.

"You better leave my woman alone, or I'm gonna whip your ass," he said. He then threw the money on the ground by Pepper's feet. "Money cain't buy you love," he shouted as everybody looked on. That settled it and nobody else ever tried to "hit on" Fannie Mae again.

Pattie Sue thought Mordecai was cute and told him so. Even though he was flattered, he told Fannie Mae. Fannie Mae, at recess, walked up to Pattie Sue and slapped her face. She then pushed her into the bushes and shouted, "That's what you get for trying to mess wit my man, bitch." Pattie Sue retaliated by getting up and grabbing Fannie's long hair. Fannie scratched Pattie's face till she let go. They grabbed each other and fell to the ground while the crowd cheered. The boys loved it because neither one of them was wearing any draws. They were separated by the principal who took both of them into his office and whipped their booties with a leather strap. They both got another whipping at home. Any girl that was attracted to Mordecai thought twice about flirting with him. From coon hunting, Fannie Mae was in too good of physical shape for any other girls to compete with, even the basketball players. They were made for each other, it seemed.

They made love whenever they wanted to because both of their parents loved and trusted them. They could go walking or riding on the ground slide unsupervised. The parents didn't know what was going on, but they had a "hankering." Sex was expected but if she became pregnant they had to marry. This Mordecai knew, so he began to use rubbers.

Because of Mordecai's strength, endurance and running and jumping skills gained from possum and coon hunting, he was recognized by the football coach who asked him to come out for the football team. He was then 11th grade and 16 years old. Indeed, he was a very good prospect as a running back and a defense back. His speed was tremendous and once he got in the open, hardly anyone could catch him. When he ran through the line, it reminded him of running through the bushes, over hills, around trees and stumps as he hunted. He was used to sidestepping and jumping over logs, so avoiding would be tacklers and crossing over players on the ground was no problem. This attracted more girls, but they didn't stand a chance. Fannie Mae attended all games and carried his helmet afterwards. Even if he thought about straying, Fannie Mae gave him no room to error. She dominated him with her presence.

* * * * *

Thomas Allison, the richest man in Hungerville, fifty-two years ago was born dirt poor in a shanty just north of the county life of Perry, in Forrest County. His family was atypical of the poor whites in his category. They only had two children, Thomas and his little sister Susanne. The other "dirt" farmers had at least six or more offspring. Their logic—the more children you have, the more hands you have to work to help get you almost out of debt and perhaps even get ahead. Very few of them ever accomplished these dreams and remained poorer than owl shit throughout death. I said throughout death because even though dead, someone had to pay the mortician and buy the burial place. Most were buried on a plot of land at home or in the church's graveyard.

Thomas could have gone to school either at Runnelstown in Perry County or at Petal. He chose Petal because that's where his girlfriend, now his wife, Peggy McAllister, lived. He met her in her daddy's cotton field and transferred from Runnelstown to Petal High. Her father, Fredrick McAllister, owned the biggest farm within a radius of 100 miles. This is where they met that summer of 1954—in one of her daddy's cotton fields picking cotton alongside the colored folks. He was eager and hungry to make money to help his ma and pa and little sister Rose. At 14 years old he could pick three hundred pounds of cotton a day. That's as much as the grown black men could pick. This was considered incredible by whites, and Thomas was given a special honor. Peggy had heard about this super white boy/man and was dying to make his acquaintance. She had seen him from a distance but never close up.

This Friday, about noon time, Peggy gave herself the job of distributing water to the workers. She had her two little Negro girls tote the ice cold water bucket while she held the dippers. They would approach the pickers and say, "Water, cool water, anybody want some?"

Everybody did want some, including Thomas Allison, who had nothing in his stomach except the possum he had eaten the night before and the biscuit with saltmeat for lunch today. There was nothing to drink at either meal, except water. The hot Mississippi sun had taken its toll on all of them and they were paying dividends in sweat. Their eyes met as she handed him the dipper first. Didn't want him to drink after the colored folks but before them. There were no paper cups, plastic cups, or Styrofoam's to choose from, only gourds for dippers. Their eyes became transfixed on each other. Their eyes approved and adored each other. Fascination or love at first sight? Who knows?

Peggy's face was as radiant as the sunshine; her smile, quaint like the Mona Lisa he had read about at Runnelstown High School, but very attractive. Her Irish freckles seemed to have been handpainted perfectly on her face by an artist to blend with her natural fiery red hair. Her face was firm and beautiful. Her bust was full with a waist that was thin. He could not see her legs because of the outfit she wore but assumed that they had to be beautiful also. He was correct.

She thought of him as Superman without his cape. His body was well proportioned with muscles competing with each other. He wore shorts and his legs were full and well proportioned. He had the smile of Clark Kent along with the dark hair in need of a combing. Why he did not wear a "sun hat" perplexed her. As she handed him the dipper, she asked, "Why don't you have a sun hat on?"

"Because I don't own one, ma'am," he replied. "The money I make picking cotton can better be spent on more important things like food and help for my ma and pa and my little sister. You see, ma'am, I'm very poor."

Peggy was stunned and fought to hold back the tears. "I'm sorry, but you shall have a sun hat Monday. What size?"

"I don't know, cause I've never even had a hat." As he drank the water, she took some ribbon from her pocket and wrapped it around his head to measure.

"You have a large head," she said as she giggled.

THE POSSUM HUNTER

He replied, "Large head, large brain. I won't be picking cotton for the rest of my life."

They both smiled. His teeth were white and beautiful enough to go with his handsome face.

Monday morning, as the pickup truck driven by her daddy stopped to unload its passengers, there stood Peggy Sue as pretty as a picture wearing shorts with a new straw hat in her hands. She approached Thomas and handed him the hat. "This is for you, my shining knight without armor."

"Thank you, Miss McAllister, but I shall pay you back. How much did it cost?" he asked.

"But I thought you were poor and have no money. How do you expect to pay me back? Accept this as a gift from the boss trying to protect an investment," she answered.

"I shall pay you back by working harder, longer, picking more cotton than I ever did before."

Peggy's father, Fred McAllister, listening, had witnessed it all and took a liking to this gallant lad. He would see that he earned more money.

When it was quitting and weighing-in time, Thomas remained in the field, picking for at least thirty minutes more. He dragged his sacks to the scales and set a record for that day—four hundred pounds!

He asked Mr. McAllister to pay him for three hundred pounds only and to give the money for the 100 pounds to his daughter for the sun hat. And if that's not enough he would do the same thing everyday until his debt was paid in full.

This noble act had caught the attention of a very wealthy man, Fredrick McAllister, and he was impressed, indeed. He had seen too many lazy persons trying to get something for nothing, both white and colored. If he were to stay in school and learn, go to Mississippi State, major in agriculture, join his Methodist church, he would consider him a viable prospect as a son-in-law and co-heir to his estate.

Fredrick McAllister had no other legal children than Fredrick Jr., Peggy, and an older daughter Rosemary. He did have "outside" children that he took care of but aren't most rich white men hypocrites and cheaters along with their wealth, charm, dignity, goodness, charity, religion, and passion?

It was rumored that two of his bastard children were colored. Well, their single mother Callie Mae Williams had electricity before everybody else in her community did. Also, she had good furniture, a gas stove, a refrigerator filled with food, and a well stocked deep freezer. She and her twins were well clothed and always clean. Did she make that much money working as his housekeeper?

If his wife Rebecca McAllister ever suspected him of infidelity, she never ever mentioned it or confronted him about it. She just kept on living the good life that her husband afforded her: one of the most beautiful houses in the state of Mississippi with colored servants to do as she willed; her own station wagon with a chauffeur if and when she ever wanted one; shopping sprees in Hattiesburg, New Orleans, Memphis, and Houston as she desired; dining with the "smart set" that included the mayor's wife, the governor's wife, Mrs. Paul B. Johnson Jr., (whom Fredrick had helped elect), the president of the Kiwanis club, the Mississippi Southern's president's wife, prominent businessmen's (like Chain and Waldoff) wives, doctor's and lawyer's spouses. She and her husband were members of both the Hattiesburg and Laurel country clubs.

So what if her husband was messing around a little as long as he didn't bring anything home like venereal diseases?

Her children were awfully fond of Callie Mae's children and treated them with love and affection. Always hugging, kissing, and giving them presents—taking them riding with them and buying them things like popcorn, peanuts, ice cream, and coca colas.

Rebecca wondered if her children knew that they may be their sister and brother. She never mentioned it. They were twins, a boy and a girl with beautiful faces and heads full of pretty curly hair. Even Rebecca thought that they were cute, though, at times, she would work the hell out of Callie Mae, giving her chores that were almost impossible to complete in the time allotted. Was she jealous?

Fredrick McAllister had several other fields of produce such as cornfields, cucumber fields, watermelon patches, peas, and another 20

THE POSSUM HUNTER

acres of cotton fields. He also planted peanuts (legumes) that he would rotate every two years with other crops, including cotton, to refurbish the soil with nitrates. This he had learned at Mississippi State where he had attended school, majoring in agriculture.

Most of the people who worked these fields were his sharecroppers. He charged them rent for living in the houses that he provided for them. The more luxuries or conveniences they required, the higher the rent. They all shopped at his mercantile store for equipment, clothing, and food. This store carried everything from gasoline, kerosene, rakes, shovels, plows, pans, pots, plants, skillets, spoons, forks, crackers, coffee and coffee cups, to milk, eggs, grits, rice, flour, bread, cheese, butter, lard, salt, pepper, sugar, flavors, spices, and meats such as ham, chicken, bacon, bologna, pork chops, neck bones, beef, and ox tails.

The store also sold wearing apparel such as aprons, dresses, shirts, suits, overalls, jeans, work shoes (brogans), caps, hats, and Sunday-go-to-meeting shoes and soft drinks. On holidays they sold whiskey and beer. If the day after the holiday was a work day, you had better be there.

No money was ever exchanged for anything, including utilities and rent. They would simply sign an IOU and be given a copy to keep for themselves. At the end of September, after all the major cotton had been harvested, each family sat down with the business person to add and subtract their profit versus their expenses.

The smart ones who actually kept their receipts and records of their products and wages would sometimes come out in the black. Most ended up owing more than their production. Even then they were never denied credit and continued to charge. They spent their lives forever indebted to the plantation owner. Fredrick McAllister ran a slave farm with unlimited credit to both whites and blacks.

The fortunate ones could sometimes afford to purchase a used car or truck and send their offspring to college. Sometimes the children, after finishing college, would find jobs that would enable them to rescue their families or parts of their families, like a younger sister or brother, and send them off to school also. They, in turn, were to continue the family rescue mission. Sooner or later, their ma's and pa's would be rescued and given a decent house to live in with means enough to now live a decent life.

With her family's approval, Peggy started dating Thomas and became his girlfriend. Thomas's parents didn't believe it. "How could a rich girl like Peggy love somebody beneath her level like Thomas?" they asked.

That next September Thomas changed schools. He transferred from Runnelstown High to Petal High. No problem, since he lived in Forrest County. Anyway, the school bus picked him up and dropped him off every day.

Mr. McAllister gave him a weekend job of tending the chickens and hogs and horses Fridays after school and all day Saturday. On Sundays he attended the Methodist church with them and soon became a member, casting aside all his Baptist upbringing. He was paid each Sunday after church $15 minus $1 for church dues. This still was a lot of money for his poor family. He and Peggy declared their love for each other and became inseparable throughout high school and were engaged during their junior year at "State." Peggy lost her virginity to Thomas their sophomore year after a panty raid.

He had met all of his future father-in-law's requirements and was accepted. He now had a job as an overseer on the McAllister's plantation and began to make hundreds of dollars. He continued to share with his family, then put the rest in a savings account at Citizens Bank in Hattiesburg. His father-in-law paid for the wedding and engagement rings with Thomas paying him all of it back.

Thomas and Peggy graduated in May from Mississippi State, she with a Bachelor's in business administration and finance and he with a Bachelor's in agriculture and finance. They were given a room in the mansion and a brand new Chevrolet sedan.

Although his diet had now changed, he still ate possum on occasion. Can you compare filet mignon to opossum?

When his father-in-law and mother-in-law passed away, they willed Thomas and Peggy a third of their estate which came to a million dollars. They moved from the family mansion into a brand new majestic plantation plaza of their own. Peggy gave birth to three children. The

THE POSSUM HUNTER

first was a daughter they named Rosemary. Two years later came Thomas Jr. and after two more years came the beautiful Suzanne.

* * * * *

Miss Thelma Louise Garrison and her daughter Pattie Sue were the kitchen folks for the Allison family. That is, they were in charge of everything in the kitchen, from cleaning it to buying the food, stocking the pantry shelves and freezers, refrigerators, to preparing the meals. Most of the times they just cooked whatever they chose. They were excellent cooks, so the Allisons eagerly awaited their meals with great anticipation. They were very seldom displeased. At times when their appetites craved certain delicacies and dishes, they would make requests that morning or the day before, giving them ample time to procure them, if it were not already in their house or yard. If they craved fresh fish, they had to be caught from their pond or go into town to the Triangle Fish Market that carried red fish, flounder, mullet, shrimp, crab, and oysters. If Mr. Allison craved opossum, they had to place an order of delivery from a possum hunter. Mordecai Johnson was their man.

Mr. and Mrs. Allison made a request for a coon or a possum feast. Pattie Sue, after having had her ass whipped by Fannie Mae before, was reluctant about talking to Mordecai again, but she had to place her order for at least a ten pound possum for her boss.

Being cautious, she approached Mordecai and Fannie Mae as they ate lunch together in the school's cafeteria, devouring their peanut butter sandwiches with soup and chocolate milk. Fannie Mae became suspicious of Pattie Sue's approach and was preparing to throw her milk into her face. She settled down when Pattie Sue spoke.

"Excuse me, y'all, but I need to place an order for a coon or possum from Mr. Allison for Mordecai if it's alright!"

"Go head," they said.

"Well, the truth of the matter be, is Mr. Fredrick wants a ten pound dressed possum or coon by Friday night if you can deliver."

S. EARL WILSON, III

"Tell him 'his will be done' by tomorrow after school if the good Lord be willing and the creeks don't rise." Mordecai had learned to talk "hep." Being such an expert hunter, he was sure that he could deliver. Fannie Mae took her eyes off of Pattie Sue and began eating again. That's when Pattie Sue blew Mordecai a kiss, smiled, and left. Mordecai was flattered but said nothing. He was beginning to "feel his oats," having two women in love with him. He didn't seem to question his loyalty to Fannie Mae.

Mordecai, continuing his hep jive talk, said to Pattie Sue, "See you later, alligator."

Pattie Sue replied, "After while, crocodile."

Fannie Mae interjected, "Pretty soon, baboon," and smiled.

Patty Sue left dejected. Was this bitch talking jive talk or was she calling her a baboon? "Time will tell as shit will smell," she thought, as she planned her revenge.

* * * * *

That day was Wednesday. By 6:00 Thursday, he carried his 11 pound possum to the Allisons. He knocked at the front door where Thelma greeted him and directed him to the back porch. She told him that colored folks and poor white folks could not come in at the front of the house. Mordecai nodded his head in acknowledgement and obliged. He was more disappointed than hurt. He had expected Pattie Sue. His disappointment was short-lived. There, on the back porch, sat Pattie on a stool with her dress above her knees, shelling peas. Her legs and part of her thighs showed. She made no attempt to pull her dress down. Mordecai liked what he saw. Her legs and thighs were beautiful and aroused him.

"Hello, Mr. Scaredy Cat," she said. "Bring the coon over here and place him on the table."

"It ain't no coon, it's a possum. And how come you called me that?"

"Called you what? Mr. Scaredy Cat? Cause you is scared of me and you is a coward that runs to Fannie Mae and tells. That's why."

"I ain't scared of you," he said.

THE POSSUM HUNTER

"You is, too," she said. "Why you peeking at my legs stead of looking at them like a real man would. Here, you wanner see mo?" she asked as she propped her feet upon a watermelon and spread her legs wide open. Mordecai was so aroused that he almost dropped the possum he carried and began to tremble and sweat. Pattie Sue stood up, took the possum, and went into the kitchen and brought him back a Coca Cola.

As she handed it to him, he asked, "What is this?"

"It's a Coke, fool, a cold drank. Ain't you ever had one befo?"

"I ain't never even seen or heard tell of one before. Is it good?" Mordecai asked.

"Drink it and see," she said.

The ice cold Coca Cola was one of the greatest gastronomical sensations and thrills that Mordecai had ever experienced. He fell instantly in love with Coca Cola.

"Now, let's get back to business. Here is your $15.00 plus $2.00 tip from Mr. Allison. Let's get back to the part where you was looking up my dress. Did you like what you saw, Scaredy Cat?"

"I don't remember what I saw. Can I see it again?"

"You shore you want to see? And you ain't gonna go back to Fannie and tell, are you?"

"Unc unca (meaning no)," he said.

"You swear?" she asked.

"I swear," he replied.

She then sat down, placed her feet again upon the watermelon, spread her legs and pulled her dress all the way up, exposing everything. She wore no bloomers. Mordecai seemed petrified and stared like a blind man who had just regained his sight. "Take a good look, honey, cause you might not ever see this again, especially if you run and tell."

"I promise you I ain't gonna tell nobody," he said.

"Well, in that case, come on over here and get a closer look and feel it."

He did. As he played with her pussy, Pattie Sue put her arms around him and kissed him, placing a yard of tongue in his mouth. That was the first time he had ever tongue kissed.

They didn't have sex because Thelma was in the kitchen, and ain't no telling when an Allison might show up. "Now, whatcha gonna do about me now, Mordecai? You have learned how to French kiss, drink Coca Cola, seen and played with my privates, squeezed and licked my titties."

"I want to go further," he said. I want to go all the way. I want to have sex with you."

"Well, maybe you can if I can be your other girlfriend. Fannie Mae can keep her role in the daytime, at school, and on Sundays. I can be your second love at nights and on Saturdays. If that's all right with you."

"It's all right with me," he said. "But how long can you stand being second?"

"As long as it takes to turn your love for me only. And I betcha that my pussy is better than hers."

"When can I find out?'

"This Saturday night. Come to my house around 8:00 at night."

He did. She was right!

* * * * *

Hungerville, Mississippi got its name from having so many "po" (poor) people. Two-thirds of its population were people of measly means, less than $2,000 a year. It wasn't really a geographical city by that name but a geographical area encompassing Forrest, Lamar, Jones, and Perry counties where most of the inhabitants were kin to each other. Blood relations crossed over county lines also.

People in Eatonville of Forrest County had kin folks in Soso in Jones County. People in New Augusta in Perry County were kin to some people just across the county line in Forrest County and into Big Creek of Jones County. Just about all people whose family's last names that were the same were related. Just about all the Fosters in south Mississippi were related. Some families even had inter-marriages, cousins marrying cousins.

So Hungerville was no particular place but a combination of places spread out. They may all have originated at a certain spot a long time ago, but little by little, some left for other areas seeking to better their lots.

THE POSSUM HUNTER

Very few did, they simply spread poverty to another location. Thomas Allison was an exception. Some sharecroppers rose to become landowners and continued the tradition of using the underprivileged to their advantages. Some were kind and generous and lent a helping hand to their poorer kinfolks. These were the religious ones who believed in God and went to church on Sundays.

Roscoe Mordecai Johnson's father and mother were not sharecroppers but almost as poor as them. His daddy's great-great granddaddy was given his freedom and a plot of land, two acres and a shanty by his owner, Colonel Lee Rumpford the second, a Civil War officer, for having fought so gallantly for the Confederacy. Yes, some blacks fought with and supported the Confederates.

This land had been in the family ever since, so they always had some place to stay, a barn, a plot of land for gardening, a pig pen, and a chicken coop. They didn't have enough land for cattle raising and not enough leftover food for raising hogs. Their gardening was poor, so they stayed hungry most of the time.

Oscar, his daddy, was a "shade tree" mechanic and a "two bits" carpenter, who hired himself out whenever and whatever the occasions demanded. He would work on automobiles, tractors, fences, churches, and houses. At times, well-to-do whites would employ him to build chicken coops, pig pens, to repair or to make additions to their houses or barns. It was he who built his son's ground slide.

When his money was good, his family ate different foods such as liver and onions and rice plus pig feet and ox tail, some bags of pig skins, peanuts, and potato chips and peppermint candy. He never purchased "soda pops" cause some people, old black folks, told him that they had a little bit of pizzon (poison) in them. Not enough to kill you right away but slowly, little by little. "That's why old man Mose went blind in one eye," they said. They didn't know it was diabetes. So he left them alone. That's why Mordecai never knew any thing about Coca Cola. Oscar would have had a fit if he had known.

Other than being almost as poor as anybody else, they were comfortable and happy most of the times. They were very religious and attended East Pine Methodist Church every first and third Sunday. You see, their preacher, Reverend Jordan, had another church on the second and fourth Sundays to serve. Sometimes the second Sunday they would attend Mt. Vernon Baptist Church. Same rituals except the Baptist people jumped and shouted and sang up tempo music a little bit more and louder. You couldn't go to sleep in their church! There was never a dull moment

Even though the high faluting colored folks and the upper class whites ate possums and coons just like the poor echelon, they sometimes cooked or had them cooked a little bit differently. The coon's meat is tougher than the opossum's, so they marinate it in pans of 7 Up or Sprite drinks. They fill the containers with 7 Up and soak the coon in it overnight in the refrigerator, sometimes longer. Then they season it as usual and roast it in the oven till it becomes golden brown and tender. The taste is often compared to chicken.

"Tastes just like chicken," said Fredrick Allison and his wife Rebecca.

"Well, then, why not have chicken?" said Suzanne and Rosemary. For them, Callie Mae and Pattie Sue fried some chicken.

Scholastically, Mordecai was no genius. He got his lessons even though he was not too fond of learning. He was somewhat studious and tried to keep up with Fannie Mae who was the epitome of erudition. She made "As" in all of her studies or classes. The threat of making anything less than an "A" sent her into shudders. She can best be described as overscrupulous. An avid reader, she forced Mordecai to try to read books and newspapers to keep abreast of things outside of their world of possums and coons and sex. Mordecai read mostly short stories like *The Rock Pile* by James Baldwin, *Marigolds* by Eugenia W. Collier, *Mules and Men* by Zora Neale Hurston. The only two books of substance that he completely read entirely were *A Tale of Two Cities* by Charles Dickens and *Black Boy* by Richard Wright. The reading of *Black Boy* would have a profound effect upon his life. He could not relate to Dickens. He struggled through but never quite understood *Macbeth* and the tragedy of *Romeo and Juliet* by William Shakespeare. Even this placed him miles ahead of most Mississippi black boys in his category.

In May of 1962, both Fannie Mae Brown and Roscoe Mordecai Johnson graduated from Springfield Consolidated High School, Route

THE POSSUM HUNTER

5, Hattiesburg, Mississippi. She as valedictorian in a class of 15 members and he as number 14. Her superior grades and test scores merited her a full scholarship to Tougaloo College in Jackson, Mississippi. Roscoe Mordecai followed her on a work and track scholarship. Tougaloo had recently abandoned football in favor of more academics. He would be accepted on probation and given a semester to prove that he could handle the strenuous academics that the school required. You see, Tougaloo is perhaps the most academic school in the state of Mississippi, including Ole Miss, Mississippi State, USM, and Millsap. The greatest academic challenge for them would be Millsap.

Upon registration, they tried to enroll in the same classes under the same instructors. They succeeded in accomplishing their schedules except for English. Mordecai would be required to take a semester of reading. His test scores indicated a reading level of an eighth grader while Fannie's was a thirteen plus.

He sat next to her or directly behind her. This was an easy arrangement so that he could peek at her answers on certain tests or that she could drop balls of paper behind her with answers. They had worked out a cheating scheme on multiple choice tests, the left hand indicated the question number, that is, one finger for number 1, two fingers for number 2, two fingers spread for 22, one finger followed by two fingers equaled number 12. On the right hand, a thumb up indicated "A," thumb across a forefinger was "B," three fingers was a C, and a closed fist was "D."

They got away with this for a year and Mordecai survived. Suspicions aroused his instructors. His grades were too high for his IQ, so they methodically placed them apart from each other and into different classes under different instructors. For her, it wasn't any problem. For him, it became "root hog or die poor pig." He was doomed to fail. In his class of government/social studies, Mordecai became enthralled with the teacher who was also the department chairman.

With the professor's help, he was doing well and had decided that this would be his major with a physical education minor. His instructor, Dr. Earnest P. Miles, Ph.D. from Princeton University, took a liking to this country boy who seemed thirsty for knowledge. He taught him, tutored him and showed him how to write correctly. Mordecai was an adept learner because he now had learned about civil rights and about Martin Luther King, Jr. A man from his hometown of Hattiesburg, Mississippi had just been elected governor of the state of Mississippi—Paul B. Johnson, Jr. He ran on the slogan "Stand Tall with Paul." This is because as lieutenant governor during the James Meredith integration effort, he stood with then Governor Ross Barnett in the middle of University Avenue defying the Supreme Court and blocked Meredith's entrance. This weighed big with the white voters and caused him to win the governorship in 1963 on the slogan "Stand Tall with Paul."

In November of 1963, the word of the death of President John F. Kennedy had no profound effect upon Mordecai and Fannie Mae. True, they knew who was president of the USA but, no, they had not come to realize his importance to them, America, and the rest of the world. They then never realized the meanings of his quotations, "Ask not what your country can do for you but what you can do for your country," or "We seek a free flow of information...We are not afraid to entrust the American people with unpleasant facts, foreign ideas, alien philosophies, and competitive values. For a nation that is afraid to let its people judge the truth and falsehood in an open market is a nation that is afraid of its people." That he was the first Catholic to hold this position meant nothing to them. They never knew about Catholicism.

They had no concept that the world had changed for the worse. They, like others in Hungerville, USA were oblivious to the world outside of them. The blacks never rode in the back of the buses, the whites never rode up front, only in the back of their own buggies, or wagons, or pickups. They never traveled on trains unless they were leaving forever for the promised lands up North. Taxis and jitneys were useless to them and eating at the back windows were things that they accepted and were accustomed to doing. Saying "Yes, Sir" and "No, Ma'am" to whites were part of their upbringing. They never had anything of value so they craved for nothing of value except for a full stomach, a place to lay their heads at night, and some money to purchase some clothes from the J.C. Penney or Sears Roebuck catalogs. If they were lucky, perhaps a mule, an automobile, or pickup truck. When their kinfolk came back home to visit from up North driving Cadillacs and Buicks, they knew that Dee-troit or Chi-Land had to be heaven.

When Malcolm X shocked the nation by referring to Kennedy's assassination as "chickens come home to roost," it had no effect on them for they knew not who he was or what he meant. He meant that President Kennedy had allured the C.I.A. to attempt to kill Fidel Castro of Cuba and this came back to haunt him. Every curse or evil act returns to its originator as chickens return to their roosts at night.

At Tougaloo they learned all of this and more. Their lives and values would change forever, and they would roost in the land of knowledge.

On the twelfth of June, 1963, both of them felt the impact of the murder of Medgar Evers in their own state. They began to hate and cried! Professor Miles cried along with them.

Paul B. Johnson, Jr. was not reelected after his term because he had fooled the ignorant white voters into believing that he was a stringent segregationist who hated the blacks. He was not. In his inaugural address, he suggested that the state of Mississippi should accept the inevitable and forget about yesteryears. At Governor Johnson's first year in office, he encouraged county officials to begin to register black voters. He had the Mississippi Legislature repeal the state's discriminatory voting laws and passed the Voting Rights Act in 1965. More blacks than ever before became registered, voters including Fannie Mae and Mordecai.

Dr. Earnest P. Miles told Mordecai that this wasn't anything new. Most of the politicians that ran for offices did not really hate the Negroes but used this to bait the poor ignorant white voters into voting for them. Those who cried "Hate the Nigger" the loudest usually won. Some even had colored offspring back home on their plantations. Mordecai immediately thought of the colored twins of Mr. McAllister back home in Hungerville.

Dr. Earnest Miles was a Caucasian professor at an all black college. He was born in Philadelphia, Pennsylvania, right up the street from the Betsy Ross house. Both his parents were Democratic school teachers who believed in life, liberty, and the pursuit of happiness for everyone.

He was taught ethics and morals at an early age and that the color of one's skin is nothing more than a color. That beneath the skin color lies a human being deserving of freedom, education, love, and equal opportunities. His parents were both members of the NAACP and fought for the cause of righteousness. Earnest couldn't count the number of crusades he had attended with his parents, with their loud and voracious voices demanding justice and equality for blacks. He remembered the numerous black leaders visiting his house, dining and drinking. One such leader was Martin Luther King, Jr. He was the one who impressed Earnest the most.

While he was a student at Princeton University pursuing his doctoral degree in political science and sociology, he went to Washington, D.C. to attend the Prayer Pilgrimage for Freedom on May 17, 1957. He wanted to gather as much firsthand information as he could for his dissertation *Perpetual Slavery 100 Years After the Emancipation Proclamation*. There he would hear one of the black national figures who had visited his house when he was a student at Penn State. He became overwhelmed with the brilliant speaker, Dr. Martin Luther King, Jr.. This is what he heard:

Give Us the Ballot

"Mr. Chairman, distinguished platform associates, fellow Americans: Three years ago the Supreme Court of this nation rendered in simple, eloquent, and unequivocal language a decision which will long be stenciled on the mental sheets of succeeding generations. For all men of goodwill, this May seventeenth decision came as a joyous daybreak to end the long night of human captivity. It came as a great beacon light of hope to millions of disinherited people throughout the world who had dared only to dream of freedom.

Unfortunately, this noble and sublime decision has not gone without opposition. This opposition has often risen to ominous proportions. Many states have risen up in open defiance. The legislative halls of the South ring loud with such words as "interposition" and "nullification."

THE POSSUM HUNTER

But even more, all types of conniving methods are still being used to prevent Negroes from becoming registered voters. The denial of this sacred right is a tragic betrayal of the highest mandates of our democratic tradition. And so our most urgent request to the president of the United States and every member of Congress is to give us the right to vote. (Yes)

Give us the ballot, and we will no longer have to worry the federal government about our basic rights.

Give us the ballot (Yes) and we will no longer plead to the federal government for passage of an anti-lynching law; we will by the power of our vote write the law on the statute books of the South (All right) and bring an end to the dastardly acts of the hooded perpetrators of violence.

Give us the ballot (Give us the ballot), and we will transform the salient misdeeds of bloodthirsty mobs (Yeah) into the calculated good deeds of orderly citizens.

Give us the ballot (Give us the ballot), and we will fill our legislative halls with men of goodwill (All right now) and send to the sacred halls of Congress men who will not sign a "Southern Manifesto" because of their devotion to the manifesto of justice. (Tell 'em about it)

Give us the ballot (Yeah), and we will place judges on the benches of the south who will do justly and love mercy (Yeah), and we will place at the head of the southern states governors who have felt not only the tang of the human, but the glow of the Divine.

Give us the ballot (Yes), and we will quietly and nonviolently, without rancor or bitterness, implement the Supreme Court's decision of May seventeenth, 1954. (That's right)

In this juncture of our nation's history, there is an urgent need for dedicated and courageous leadership. If we are to solve the problems ahead and make racial justice a reality, this leadership must be fourfold.

First, there is a need for strong, aggressive leadership from the federal government. So far, only the judicial branch of the government has evinced this quality of leadership. If the executive and legislative branches of the government were as concerned about the protection of our citizenship rights as the federal courts have been, then the transition from a segregated to an integrated society would be infinitely smoother. But we so often look to Washington in vain for this concern. In the midst of the tragic breakdown of law and order, the executive branch of the government is all too silent and apathetic. In the midst of the desperate need for civil rights legislation, the legislative branch of the government is all too stagnant and hypocritical.

This dearth of positive leadership from the federal government is not confined to one particular political party. Both political parties have betrayed the cause of justice. (Oh yes) The Democrats have betrayed it by capitulating to the prejudices and undemocratic practices of the southern Dixiecrats. The Republicans have betrayed it by capitulating to the blatant hypocrisy of right wing, reactionary northerners. These men so often have a high blood pressure of words and an anemia of deeds. (laughter)

In the midst of these prevailing conditions, we come to Washington today pleading with the president and members of Congress to provide a strong, moral, and courageous leadership for a situation that cannot permanently be evaded. We come humbly to say to the men in the forefront of our government that the civil rights issue is not an Ephemeral, evanescent domestic issue that can be kicked about by reactionary guardians of the status quo; it is rather an eternal moral issue which may well determine the destiny of our nation (Yes) in the ideological struggle with communism. The hour is late. The clock of destiny is ticking out. We must act now, before it is too late.

A second area in which there is need for strong leadership is from the white northern liberals. There is a dire need today for a liberalism which is truly liberal. What we are witnessing today in so many northern communities is a sort of quasi-liberalism so bent on seeing all sides, that it fails to become committed to either side. It is a liberalism that is so objectively analytical that it is not subjectively committed. It is a liberalism which is neither hot nor cold, but lukewarm. (All right) We call for a liberalism from the North which will be thoroughly committed to the ideal of racial justice and will not be deterred by the propaganda and subtle words of those who say: "Slow up for a while; you're pushing too fast."

THE POSSUM HUNTER

A third source that we must look to for strong leadership is from the moderates of the white South. It is unfortunate that at this time the leadership of the white South stems from the close-minded reactionaries. These persons gain prominence and power by the dissemination of false ideas and by deliberately appealing to the deepest hate responses within the human mind. It is my firm belief that this close-minded, reactionary, recalcitrant group constitutes a numerical minority. There are in the white South more open-minded moderates than appears on the surface. These persons are silent today because of fear of social, political, and economic reprisals. God grant the white moderates of the South will rise up courageously, without fear, and take up the leadership in this tense period of transition.

I cannot close without stressing the urgent need for strong, courageous and intelligent leadership from the Negro community. We need a leadership that is calm and yet positive. This is no day for the rabble-rouser, whether he be Negro or white. (All right) We must realize that we are grappling with the most weighty social problem of this nation, and in grappling with such a complex problem there is no place for misguided emotionalism. (All right, That's right) We must work passionately and unrelentingly for the goal of freedom, but we must be sure that our hands are clean in the struggle. We must never struggle with falsehood, have, or malice. We must never become bitter. I know how we feel sometime. There is the danger that those of us who have been forced so long to stand amid the tragic midnight of oppression—those of us who have been trampled over, those of us who have been kicked about—there is the danger that we will become bitter. But if we will become bitter and indulge in hate campaigns, the new order which is emerging will be nothing but a duplication of the old order. (Yeah, That's all right)

We must meet hate with love. We must meet physical force with soul force. (Yeah) There is still a voice crying out through the vista of time, saying: "Love your enemies (Yeah), bless them that curse you (Yes), pray for them that despitefully use you." (That's right. All right) Then, and only then, can you matriculate into the university of eternal life. That same voice cries out in terms lifted to cosmic proportions: "He who lives by the sword will perish by the sword." (Yes, Lord) And history is replete with the bleached bones of nations (Yeah) that failed to follow this command. (All right) We must follow nonviolence and love. (Yes, Lord)

Now, I'm not talking about a sentimental, shallow kind of love. (Go ahead) I'm not talking about *eros*, which is a sort of aesthetic, romantic love. I'm not even talking about *philla*, which is a sort of intimate affection between personal friends. But I'm talking about *agape*. (Yes sir) I'm talking about the love of God in the hearts of men. (Yes) I'm talking about a type of love which will cause you to love the person who does the evil deed while hating the deed that the person does. (Go ahead) We've got to love. (Oh yes)

There is another warning signal. We talk a great deal about our rights, and rightly so. We proudly proclaim that three-fourths of the peoples of the world are colored. We have the privilege of noticing in our generation the great drama of freedom and independence as it unfolds in Asia and Africa. All of these things are in line with the unfolding work of Providence. But we must be sure that we accept them in the right spirit. We must not seek to use our emerging freedom and our growing power to do the same thing to the white minority that has been done to us for so many centuries. (Yes) Our aim must never be to defeat or humiliate the white man. We must not become victimized with a philosophy of black supremacy. God is not interested merely in freeing black men and brown men and yellow men, but God is interested in freeing the whole human race. (Yes, All right) We must work with determination to create a society (Yes), not where black men are superior and other men are inferior and vice versa, but a society in which all men will live together as brothers (Yes) and respect the dignity and worth of human personality. (Yes)

We must also avoid the temptation of being victimized with a psychology of victors. We have won marvelous victories. Through the work of the NAACP, we have been able to do some of the most amazing things of this generation. And I come this afternoon with nothing but praise for this great organization, the work that it has already done and the work that it will do in the future. And although they're

THE POSSUM HUNTER

outlawed in Alabama and other states, the fact still remains that this organization has done more to achieve civil rights for Negroes than any other organization we can point to. (Yeah, amen) Certainly, this is fine. But we must not, however, remain satisfied with a court victory over our white brothers. We must respond to every decision with an understanding of those who have opposed us and with an appreciation of the difficult adjustments that the court orders pose for them. We must act in such a way as to make possible a coming together of white people and colored people on the basis of a real harmony of interest and understanding. We must seek an integration based on mutual respect.

I conclude by saying that each of us must keep faith in the future. Let us not despair. Let us realize that as we struggle for justice and freedom, we have cosmic companionship. This is the long faith of the Hebraic-Christian tradition: that God is not some Aristotelian Unmoved Mover who merely contemplates upon himself. He is not merely a self-knowing God, but an other-loving God (Yeah) forever working through history for the establishment of His kingdom.

And those of us who call the name of Jesus Christ find something of an event in our Christian faith that tells us this. There is something in our faith that says to us, "Never despair: never give up: never feel that the cause of righteousness and justice is doomed." There is something in our Christian faith, at the center of it, which says to us that Good Friday may occupy the throne for a day, but ultimately it must give way to the triumphant beat of the drums of Easter. (That's right) There is something in our faith that says evil may so shape events, that Caesar will occupy the palace and Christ the cross (That's right), but one day that same Christ will rise up and split history into a.d. and b.c. (Yes), so that even the life of Caesar must be dated by his name. (Yes)

There is something in this universe (Yes, Yes) which justifies Carlyle in saying: "No lie can live forever." (All right) There is something in this universe which justifies William Cullen Bryant in saying: "Truth crushed to earth will rise again." (Yes, All right) There is something in this universe (Watch yourself) which justifies James Russell Lowell in saying:

S. EARL WILSON, III

Truth forever on the scaffold,
Wrong forever on the throne. (Oh yeah)
Yet that scaffold sways the future,
And behind the dim unknown
Stands God (All right), within the shadow,
Keeping watch above His own. (Yeah, yes)

Go out with that faith today. (All right, Yes) Go back to your homes in the Southland to that faith, with that faith today. Go back to Philadelphia, to New York, to Detroit and Chicago with that faith today (That's right): that the universe is on our side in the struggle. (Sure is, Yes) Stand up for justice. (Yes)

Sometimes it gets hard, but it is always difficult to get out of Egypt, for the Red Sea always stands before you with discouraging dimensions. (Yes) And even after you've crossed the Red Sea, you have to move through a wilderness with prodigious hilltops of evil (Yes) and gigantic mountains of opposition. (Yes) But I say to you this afternoon: Keep moving. (Go on ahead) Let nothing slow you up. (Go on ahead) Move on with dignity and honor and respectability. (Yes)

I realize that it will cause restless nights sometimes. It might cause losing a job: it will cause suffering and sacrifice. (That's right) It might even cause physical death for some. But if physical death is the price that some must pay (Yes sir) to free their children from a permanent life of psychological death (Yes sir), then nothing can be more Christian. (Yes sir) Keep going today. (Yes sir) Keep moving amid every obstacle. (Yes sir) Keep moving amid every mountain of opposition. (Yes, sir, Yeah) If you will do that with dignity (Say it), when the history books are written in the future, the historians will have to look back and say, "There lived a great people. (Yes sir, Yes) A people with 'fleecy locks and black complexion (Yes),' but a people who injected new meaning into the veins of civilization; a people which stood up with dignity and honor and saved Western civilization in her darkest hour (Yes); a people that gave new integrity and a new dimension of love to our civilization." (Yeah, Look out) When that happens, "the morning stars will sing together, (Yes, sir) and the sons of God will shout for joy." (Yes, sir, All right)

Although, already a liberal, Dr. Earnest P. Miles, after hearing this great oratory, rededicated himself to the cause. Martin Luther King, Jr. was adored by him to the point of idolatry. He would serve and follow him. He chose Mississippi. He chose Tougaloo College. Tougaloo was honored to have such a scholar asking to become a member of their faculty. The salary didn't even come close to what he would have gotten at Harvard, Smith, or Yale.

His sympathy for Mordecai caused him to render him help rather than judge him on the basis of test scores. He had read about the poor impoverished black people of Mississippi and decided to do something about them. With his concern, help and sympathy, Mordecai became a C+ to B- student without the help of Fannie Mae. The passion that Professor Miles felt for Dr. Martin Luther King, Jr. flowed over into Mordecai as well. They both became worshippers.

Even though Mordecai joined in and sat in demonstrations in Jackson and across the state, Fannie Mae did not follow him. She was satisfied with joining the NAACP and attending local meetings on campus including SNCC, the student non-violence coordinating committee. The practice of non violence wasn't in her genes although she had read about and admired Mahatma Gandhi. If she would slap any girl who flirted with her man and had not touched her, what would she do if she sat at a counter and somebody poured ketchup in her hair? Kick ass!

Martin Luther King, Jr. was a driving force for equality and justice for blacks. So much so that he was often arrested and thrown into jail. He never fought back. He held dear the principles of non violence. In 1963 he spearheaded a march upon the nation's capital to make demands to end racial segregation in public schools, employment, to protect civil rights workers from being beaten by police, and a $2.00 minimum wage for all workers.

The march was highly successful. More than a quarter million people of different races, ethics, backgrounds, and religions attended from all across the USA. It was the largest number of people of protest in

S. EARL WILSON, III

Washington's history. Among this mass of human beings were Mordecai Johnson and the person who brought him there, Dr. Earnest P. Miles, his professor. He had driven his car to Hattiesburg, Mississippi, visited Mordecai's home, met his family, then caught the railroad train from Hattiesburg to D.C. Being white, Dr. Miles found excellent accommodations to stay. This was a brand new experience for Mordecai, staying in a Holiday Inn and eating sirloin steaks. Something like his first introduction to Coca Cola. "We live and learn." He thought about Pattie Sue.

When the waiter asked him how he enjoyed his steak, he replied, "Better than possum but almost as good as coon." Dr. Miles was aghast, horrified at the answer, but the waiter understood and smiled. He was from Tuskegee, Alabama.

This marked the introduction of Mordecai and his date Fannie Mae to various foods outside their vernacular and provided by Dr. Miles who thought it was his duty to help transform the minds of the underprivileged, including their eating habits. They were introduced to pancakes and syrup that they thought were hoe cakes and molasses. They ate shrimp, oysters, fish fillet, broccoli, asparagus, prime rib, spaghetti and pastas, pizza, hot dogs, sundaes, floats and strawberry shortcakes, cantaloupes and honeydew melons, lamb, hor d'ourves, cheeses, and Chinese foods. In all their tastings, they never found a food that they didn't like. This pleased their host to the utmost.

They learned about wine, whiskey, and beer from the other students on campus. They both got drunk the first time but never again. Tougaloo was a party school also.

Aside from the train ride, the hotel stay, the food they ate, the gathering of thousands of people of all nationalities, the highlight of the trip was the *I Have a Dream* speech by their idol, Dr. Martin Luther King, Jr., regarded along with Abraham Lincoln's Gettysburg Address as one of the finest speeches in America's oratory history. This is what they heard:

"I am happy to join with you today in what will go down in history as the greatest demonstration for freedom in the history of our nation.

THE POSSUM HUNTER

Five score years ago, a great American, in whose symbolic shadow we stand today, signed the Emancipation Proclamation. This momentous decree came as a great beacon light of hope to millions of Negro slaves who had been seared in the flames of withering injustice. It came as a joyous daybreak to end the long night of their captivity.

But one hundred years later, the Negro still is not free. One hundred years later, the life of the Negro is still sadly crippled by the manacles of segregation and the chains of discrimination. One hundred years later, the Negro lives on a lonely island of poverty in the midst of a vast ocean of material prosperity. One hundred years later, the Negro is still languishing in the corners of American society and finds himself an exile in his own land. So we have come here today to dramatize a shameful condition.

In a sense we have come to our nation's capital to cash a check. When the architects of our republic wrote the magnificent words of the Constitution and the Declaration of Independence, they were signing a promissory note to which every American was to fall heir. This note was a promise that all men, yes, black men as well as white men, would be guaranteed the unalienable rights of life, liberty, and the pursuit of happiness.

It is obvious today that America has defaulted on this promissory note insofar as her citizens of color are concerned. Instead of honoring this sacred obligation, America has given the Negro people a bad check, a check which has come back marked "insufficient funds." But we refuse to believe that the bank of justice is bankrupt. We refuse to believe that there are insufficient funds in the great vaults of opportunity of this nation. So we have come to cash this check—a check that will give us upon demand the riches of freedom and the security of justice. We have also come to this hallowed spot to remind America of the fierce urgency of now. This is no time to engage in the luxury of cooling off or to take the tranquilizing drug of gradualism. Now is the time to make real the promises of democracy. Now is the time to rise from the dark and desolate valley of segregation to the sunlit path of racial justice. Now is the time to lift our nation from the quick sands of racial injustice to the solid rock of brotherhood. Now is the time to make justice a reality for all of God's children.

It would be fatal for the nation to overlook the urgency of the moment. This sweltering summer of the Negro's legitimate discontent will not pass until there is an invigorating autumn of freedom and equality. Nineteen sixty-three is not an end, but a beginning. Those who hope that the Negro needed to blow off steam and will be content will have a rude awakening if the nation returns to business as usual. There will be neither rest nor tranquility in America until the Negro is granted his citizenship rights. The whirlwinds of revolt will continue to shake the foundations of our nation until the bright day of justice emerges.

But there is something that I must say to my people who stand on the warm threshold which leads into the palace of justice. In the process of gaining our rightful place we must not be guilty of wrongful deeds. Let us not seek to satisfy our thirst for freedom by drinking from the cup of bitterness and hatred.

We must forever conduct our struggle on the high plane of dignity and discipline. We must not allow our creative protest to degenerate into physical violence. Again and again we must rise to the majestic heights of meeting physical force with soul force. The marvelous new militancy which has engulfed the Negro community must not lead us to distrust of all white people, for many of our white brothers, as evidenced by their presence here today, have come to realize that their destiny is tied up with our destiny and their freedom is inextricably bound to our freedom. We cannot walk alone.

As we walk, we must make the pledge that we shall march ahead. We cannot turn back. There are those who are asking the devotees of civil rights, "When will you be satisfied?" We can never be satisfied as long s the Negro is the victim of the unspeakable horrors of police brutality. We can never be satisfied, as long as our bodies, heavy with the fatigue of travel, cannot gain lodging in the motels of the highways and the hotels of the cities. We can never be satisfied as long as a Negro in Mississippi cannot vote and a Negro in New York believes he has nothing for which to vote. No, no, we are not satisfied, and we will not be satisfied until justice rolls down like waters and righteousness like a mighty stream.

I am not unmindful that some of you have come here out of great trials and tribulations. Some of you have come fresh from narrow jail cells. Some of you have come from areas where your quest for freedom left you battered by the storms of persecution and staggered by the winds of police brutality. You have been the veterans of creative suffering. Continue to work with the faith that unearned suffering is redemptive.

Go back to Mississippi, go back to Alabama, go back to South Carolina, go back to Georgia, go back to Louisiana, go back to the slums and ghettos of our northern cities, knowing that somehow this situation can and will be changed. Let us not wallow in the valley of despair.

I say to you today, my friends, so even though we face the difficulties of today and tomorrow. I still have a dream. It is a dream deeply rooted in the American dream.

I have a dream that one day this nation will rise up and live out the true meaning of its creed: "We hold these truths to be self-evident: that all men are created equal."

I have a dream that one day on the red hills of Georgia the sons of former slaves and the sons of former slave owners will be able to sit down together at the table of brotherhood.

I have a dream that one day even the state of Mississippi, a state sweltering with the heat of injustice, sweltering with the heat of oppression, will be transformed into an oasis of freedom and justice.

I have a dream that my four little children will one day live in a nation where they will not be judged by the color of their skin but by the content of their character.

I have a dream today.

I have a dream that one day, down in Alabama, with its vicious racists, with its governor having his lips dripping with the words of interposition and nullification; one day right there in Alabama, little black boys and black girls will be able to join hands with little white boys and white girls as sisters and brothers.

S. EARL WILSON, III

I have a dream today.

I have a dream that one day every valley shall be exalted, every hill and mountain shall be made low, the rough places will be made plain, and the crooked places will be made straight, and the glory of the Lord shall be revealed, and all flesh shall see it together.

This is our hope. This is the faith that I go back to the South with. With this faith we will be able to hew out of the mountain of despair a stone of hope. With this faith we will be able to transform the jangling discords of our nation into a beautiful symphony of brotherhood. With this faith we will be able to work together, to pray together, to struggle together, to go to jail together, to stand up for freedom together, knowing that we will be free one day.

This will be the day when all of God's children will be able to sing with a new meaning, "My country, 'tis of thee, sweet land of liberty, of thee I sing. Land where my fathers died, land of the pilgrim's pride, from every mountainside, let freedom ring."

And if America is to be a great nation this must become true. So let freedom ring from the prodigious hilltops of New Hampshire. Let freedom ring from the mighty mountains of New York. Let freedom ring from the heightening Alleghenies of Pennsylvania!

Let freedom ring from the snowcapped Rockies of Colorado!

Let freedom ring from the curvaceous slopes of California!

But not only that, let freedom ring from Stone Mountain of Georgia!

Let freedom ring from Lookout Mountain of Tennessee!

Let freedom ring from every hill and molehill of Mississippi. From every mountainside, let freedom ring.

And when this happens. When we allow freedom to ring, when we let it ring from every village and every hamlet, from every state and every city, we will be able to speed up that day when all of God's children, black men and white men, Jews and Gentiles, Protestants and Catholics, will be able to join hands and sing in the words of the old Negro spiritual, "Free at last! free at last! thank God Almighty, we are free at last!"

* * * * *

Mordecai and Fannie Mae became enthralled with seeing and meeting dignitaries—people outside of their accustomed realms of par and below par.

They admired the campus speakers and at times tried to say hello to them. If they were acknowledged in any manner, they would be appreciative.

Muhammad Ali, then Cassius Clay, in 1963 visited his cousin James Norwood on Tougaloo's campus where he was introduced to Fannie Mae and Mordecai. He was the first celebrity that they had ever met. Fannie Mae, along with other girls tried to flirt, but I guess her complexion was too dark for him. Mordecai got jealous and thought about challenging him. I wonder who would have won?

Muhammad Ali

Muhammad Ali (born Cassius Marcellus Clay Jr. on January 17, 1942) was a three-time World Heavyweight Champion and winner of an Olympic Light-Heavyweight gold medal. He was crowned "Sportsman Of the Century" by *Sports Illustrated* and the BBC.

S. EARL WILSON, III

Ali was born in Louisville, Kentucky. He was named after his father, Cassius Marcellus Clay Sr., who was named for the 19th century abolitionist and politician Cassius Clay. Ali changed his name after joining the Nation of Islam in 1964 and subsequently converted to Islam in 1975.

Name Muhammad Ali
Birth name Cassius Marcellus Clay Jr.
Nickname The Greatest; The Champ; The Louisville Lip
Height 1.91 m (6 ft. 3 in.)
Reach 2 m
Weight division Heavyweight
Religion Muslim
Nationality United States
Ethnicity African-American
Birthdate January 17, 1942
Birthplace Louisville, Kentucky, U.S.
Stance Orthodox

Boxing record

Total fights 61
Wins 56
Wins by KO 37
Losses 5
Draws 0
No contests 0

* * * * *

College life brings new acquaintances and temptations that can disrupt vows, pledges, and faithfulness thought to be as solid as the Rock of Gibraltar. Mordecai became attracted to a young coed named Bessie Mae Graham from Tupelo, Mississippi in his sociology class. She was cute and bright, not only in color but also in mind. Mordecai was used to seeking the help of smart females, so he attached himself to her. Also, like him, she too was a member of the NAACP.

On a bus ride returning from a demonstration in Canton, Mississippi, they sat by each other. It was brutal, and they had physically been beaten. Bessie had been pushed from a counter by a white girl and had injured her knee which was slightly swollen. She complained of her discomfort to Mordecai who immediately examined her knee and went up front to the ice chest to get her some ice. He wrapped the ice in a towel, then applied it to her knee. His concern and actions impressed Bessie Mae indeed. He had learned this from having played high school football. Her knees and legs were beautiful. She had been declared "the girl with the prettiest legs on campus" by all fraternities and most all males, including the professors who would secretly look when she wore short skirts in their classes. Bessie knew well how beautiful her legs were and took advantage of her gifts from God. Professors were forgiven for touching her legs when she went to them for extra help if they promised her good grades. She would permit them to feel and rub her legs and even let them kiss her but nothing else. She never made a grade lower than a B+ and complained about that. Sometimes the professor would go back and change the grade to an A-.

This act by Mordecai touched her sincerely and she thanked him by kissing him. She stuck her tongue in his mouth just like Patty Sue did. Immediately, he fell out of, and into, love at the same time.

Bessie Mae and the entire campus knew about the relationship between Mordecai and his "home girl" Fannie Mae. So they met secretly at first. When she knew she had Mordecai's nose opened (in love), she demanded an open relationship.

Mordecai was troubled. He didn't know how to break the news to and how to break up with Fannie whom he felt devoted to and didn't want to hurt. He promised Bessie that he would tell Fannie that night and tomorrow they would walk the campus openly, holding hands.

Mordecai and Fannie met that evening at the school's canteen. There he would tell her the news that would break her heart, he thought.

S. EARL WILSON, III

Fannie Mae was used to Mordecai's inept mind and country way of speaking but considered them acceptable for the man that she had chosen to marry. She had met Fred Woullard from New York, New York in her history class and, at first, felt guilty about her attraction to him. She suppressed her desires for him. He was handsome with "good hair," keen features and smarter than anyone in their classes. He spoke eloquently with a New York Yankee brough that fascinated all of the southern girls. The only girl that intrigued him was Fannie Mae. Her southern drawl and most intelligent mind perplexed him. How can anyone talk so country and possess such a remarkable mind? He was also in another class with her, calculus, and she had the highest grade. Was she some kind of freak? And, man, was she good looking with pretty legs and full bosom with a smile that would melt ice cream!

What drew them together was an assignment given to them both. They had been pre-selected by their history professor, Dr. Charles Taylor, Ph.D.—Harvard University, B.A.—Tougaloo College, to work together. He separated his students into pairs to compete for writing about people who have contributed to our modern day way of thinking about the past and reshaping our thought and philosophies of today.

This pair of Woullard and Brown were selected to research and write about India-born Eric Blair, an Englishman educated at Eton. Eric Blair, alias George Orwell, had a knack for humbug and a genius for exposing it. He was peeved at the super-humbug of totalitarianism and wrote to awaken others about it. They would use his books *1984*, *Animal Farm* and *Coming Up for Air* as their basis.

Fannie Mae and Mordecai met at the entrance to the canteen. As they entered, the jukebox was blasting away with Bobby Blue Bland's voice singing, "And when you got a heartache, ain't nothing you can do."

Mordecai felt remorseful about what he was about to do. He still cared for Fannie Mae and about her feelings, but his new love conquered and dominated him completely. While meeting secretly, they had gone to a rooming house to make love. For the first time in all his lovemaking, they both removed all of their clothings and made love on a comfortable bed. He had never seen Fannie Mae completely naked. Well, almost, except for that time they went to the swimming hole and

THE POSSUM HUNTER

she removed everything except her draws. Even then, there was no bed and they made love on the ground.

They sat alone together, away from the crowd, away from the jukebox where couples danced and talked and sang, ate skins, chips, candy along with drinking their Cokes or root beers or 7 Ups, while chewing Juicy Fruit chewing gum or Spearmint gum. Mordecai had bought two Cokes and a bag of pig skins for them with some hot sauce.

After a conversation about folks back home in Hungerville, civil rights, and campus life, Mordecai said, "Fannie Mae, there is something I have to tell you, and it hurts my heart to do so but it's got to be done, I promise."

Fannie Mae, bracing herself for what she already suspected, said, "Well, what you got to say?" Tougaloo is a small college and gossip spreads at the speed of light all across the campus. She had already heard about Bessie Mae and Mordecai, but it didn't matter because she was planning to tell him about Fred Woullard and didn't quite know how to tell him for fear of breaking his heart or him "jumping on" Fred.

You see, in the midst of Fred and Fannie's research, they had gone into Jackson in Fred's Volkswagen to use the library at Millsap College. They did their work and checked out the two books that they needed. They already had one, *Coming Up for Air*, from Tougaloo's library. On the way back to campus, Fred took a back route. He pulled his car up into a secluded spot between trees off of Hanging Moss Road and lit a cigarette. He offered Fannie Mae one, but she smiled and said, "No, thank you. I don't smoke." He then took out another Lucky Strike, put it into his mouth, and lit it. He then placed the burning cigarette into Fannie's mouth and taught her how to smoke. She gagged at first but learned how to smoke. He reached inside his glove compartment and pulled out two paper cups and a half pint of Jack Daniels whiskey. Fred reached underneath his seat and brought forth a Coca Cola. He mixed both of them a drink, pouring mostly Coke in hers, and taught her how to drink alcohol. The two wrong things that she had recently learned, she enjoyed them both immensely, smoking and drinking.

After the second drink, mostly Coca Cola in hers, he then placed his hands on her shoulders, pulled her towards him, and kissed her lips. This was her third thrill for the night! I know that Mordecai claims you for himself, but I want you for myself," he said. "Do you think I have a chance?" he asked. "I think I love you and I don't want my love to be lost or wasted. But if my love for you is in vain, then, as the poet says, 'tis better to have loved and lost than never to have loved at all.'

She was intrigued. "Fred, I have been in love with you ever since I first saw you and heard you speak. I thought all of my love was reserved for Mordecai but now I'm not sure anymore."

They tongue kissed as he slid his left hand under her dress towards her panties while his right hand unbuckled her brassiere. With her help, Fred was successful in removing them both. They made passionate love in the small Volkswagen. They were not comfortable but gratified to the utmost. Her pleasure overshadowed her feelings of guilt. They met secretly, having even more sexual encounters and Fannie Mae was completely "hooked" on cigarettes, Jack Daniels, and Fred. She wondered how to tell Mordecai.

She breathed a sigh of relief when Mordecai said, "Fannie Mae, the fact of the matter be—"

"Not be," Fannie Mae interrupted. "Is, is! You are a college student now, not a bumpkin from Hungerville anymore." Comparing his diction with Fred's irked her to the utmost.

Mordecai continued to diminish in stature. He continued. "The fact of the matter is—is that I'm in love wit somebody else now, and I needs to break up with you. I gotta put you down." Tears fell from both of their eyes, and Mordecai cried like a baby.

Fannie Mae stood up, took Mordecai by the hand, kissed his cheek and said, "Do you really love her, and are you sure that she loves you?"

"Yes," he said.

"Then all is fair. I shall not hold you back. We've had our good times together. She then quoted Shakespeare:

But love is blind, and lovers cannot see
The pretty follies that themselves commit.

THE POSSUM HUNTER

Who knows, perhaps somewhere in the future we will meet again. Goodbye!" She kissed him upon his lips and left. Mordecai didn't even understand anything she said except "Goodbye." His crying ceased as he breathed a sigh of relief.

He then went to Bessie Mae who sat alone in a booth awaiting his arrival. He took with him his Coke and the pig skins, then ordered another Coke for Bessie.

Oh, now, the sheep have been released from their shed to graze and mingle in the open pasture! While in the shed they only had each other. In the open pasture, there was lots and lots of room to graze, along with many other sheep to choose to associate and mingle with. Mordecai and Fannie Mae were like sheep in a shed that had only each other. Both of them had many admirers who were hesitant or reluctant to "hit on" or make a pass at either of them, unlike Fred or Bessie. When their bond was broken, they became "open season" for all admirers. These new relationships would be filled with temptation and tested seriously.

There were females who disliked Fannie because of her good looks. There were those who hated her because of her brains. There were those who were jealous of her and wanted Mordecai's attention.

Mordecai's fan club was bigger than he could imagine. He didn't even know he had a fan club. Fannie's fan club multiplied enormously. She became the Kappa Alpha Psi's sweetheart, homecoming queen, president of the student body, a member of the Delta Sigma Theta sorority, the Honor Society, and a member of the president's list.

In spite of their newfound popularity, neither of them ever strayed fully. There were times when temptations were so intriguing that they may have yielded temporarily, but never enough to leave their new partners.

Tougaloo was filled with beautiful people, both male and female. There was this beautiful high yellow girl whose father was a white plantation owner in Greenwood who came over to Mordecai at a dance in Steven's Rose Room in Jackson, slightly high off of vodka and orange juice. Bessie Mae had gone home that weekend so he was there alone with some of his fraternity brothers. He was now a "Q" (Omega). He had seen her on campus but never had a conversation with her. Her name was not a typical Negro girl's name. It was Gizelle J. Haniford. The "J" stood for Juanita. Gizelle was one of the prettiest girls, not only on Tougaloo's campus but in Jackson, Mississippi as well. She was pretty. She was wealthy and her father was white. She had her pick of men and often dropped them like hot potatoes when she grew tired of them.

Gizelle approached Mordecai's table with two Screwdrivers (drinks) in her hands. One she gave to Mordecai. She said to him, "Drink this, then come dance with me." He swallowed the vodka and orange juice while she finished her drink and placed her empty glass upon his table. He arose and began to dance with Gizelle.

Mordecai was an excellent dancer and so was Gizelle. She had had dancing lessons since the age of three, ballet included. It was a fast piece and they stole the show while other dancers stopped dancing and cheered them on. Gizelle enjoyed the attention and the spotlight. The lights started to become dimmer as the band from Vicksburg began to play slower, softer with their female vocalist singing *Stardust*. This brought them closer together with their bodies rubbing each other sensually, symmetrically. They were "hot" for each other.

Gizelle then ordered two more rounds of drinks for his fraternity brothers. Paid for them, then departed with Mordecai on her arm. She drove her brand new Thunderbird to a newly integrated motel in downtown Jackson where she already had her room. In her room as she began to undress, she said to Mordecai, "I've been looking at you for quite some time and thought I would like to know just what you are all about sexually. I warn you—I don't fall in love easily, so don't you fall in love with me. Tonight is just an experiment. I may never speak to you again and then again, I might. I'm not looking for a relationship, and neither should you. But you already have one, don't you?"

"Why me?" he asked.

"Because you are popular and handsome and other girls want you."

No more words were spoken. They took off their clothes, kissed, fondled each other, and made love until she could stand no more. Mordecai established himself as a lover and, yes, she would see him again but only to make love secretly.

THE POSSUM HUNTER

* * * * *

The summer of 1964, Freedom Summer, affected Mordecai terrifically, immensely. He winced, aghast at the cruelty and horrifying events of murder in his state. He felt pity and cried for the two white and one black civil rights volunteers who had come to Mississippi to help register black voters. They were Andrew Goodman (white), Michael Schwerner (white), and James Chaney (black).

All three were murdered, and their bodies were hidden in an earthen dam. Local law enforcement agents had participated in this hideous, ghastly crime.

Now Mordecai was a churchgoing Christian who did not believe in hate. He had heard a quote by Booker T. Washington that he had relished—"I will let no man drag me so low as to make me hate him." Mordecai didn't want to hate but he had been driven to the boiling point of hate only to be retrieved by the voice and actions of the President of the United States, Lyndon B. Johnson. President Johnson ordered work begun on a voting rights bill in 1964, and in 1965, he asked Congress for the measure in his famous, perhaps his greatest, State of the Union address in January 1965. Congress stalled and that's when Martin Luther King, Jr. led a march on Selma, Alabama. Alabama officials were monstrous and brutal in their attack on the demonstrators. They beat, kicked, dragged, stomped, and murdered some of the marchers. The whole thing was televised all across America. Such monstrous acts of violence had never been seen in this country before. These barbaric, savage, inhuman acts sickened the country, causing thousands to head to the South to join Dr. King.

Here is President Johnson's speech:

The American Promise
Mr. Speaker, Mr. President, Members of the Congress:
I speak tonight for the dignity of man and the destiny of democracy.
I urge every member of both parties, Americans of all religions and of all colors, from every section of this country, to join me in that cause.

S. EARL WILSON, III

At times history and fate meet at a single time in a single place to shape a turning point in man's unending search for freedom. So it was at Lexington and Concord. So it was a century ago at Appomattox. So it was last week in Selma, Alabama. There, long-suffering men and women peacefully protested the denial of their rights as Americans. Many were brutally assaulted. One good man, a man of God, was killed.

There is no cause for pride in what has happened in Selma. There is no cause for self-satisfaction in the long denial of equal rights of millions of Americans. But there is cause for hope and for faith in our democracy in what is happening here tonight.

For the cries of pain and the hymns and protests of oppressed people have summoned into convocation all the majesty of this great Government—the Government of the greatest Nation on earth.

Our mission is at once the oldest and the most basic of this country: to right wrong, to do justice, to serve man.

In our time we have come to live with moments of great crisis. Our lives have been marked with debate about great issues; issues of war and peace, issues of prosperity and depression. But rarely in any time does an issue lay bare the secret heart of America itself. Rarely are we met with a challenge, not to our growth or abundance, our welfare or our security, but rather to the values and the purposes and the meaning of our beloved Nation.

The issue of equal rights for American Negroes is such an issue. And should we defeat every enemy, should we double our wealth and conquer the stars, and still be unequal to this issue, then we will have failed as a people and as a nation.

For with a country as with a person, "What is a man profited, if he shall gain the whole world, and lose his own soul?"

There is no Negro problem. There is no Southern problem. There is no Northern problem. There is only an American problem. And we are met here tonight as Americans—not as Democrats or Republicans—we are met here as Americans to sole that problem.

This was the first nation in the history of the world to be founded with a purpose. The great phrases of that purpose still sound in every American heart, North and South. "All men are created equal"— "government by consent of the governed"— "give me liberty or give me death." Well, those are not just clever words, or those are not just empty theories. In their name Americans have fought and died for two

THE POSSUM HUNTER

centuries, and tonight around the world they stand there as guardians of our liberty, risking their lives.

Those words are a promise to every citizen that he shall share in the dignity of man. This dignity cannot be found in a man's possessions; it cannot be found in his power, or in his position. It really rests on his right to be treated as a man equal in opportunity to all others. It says that he shall share in freedom, he shall choose his leaders, educate his children, and provide for his family according to his ability and his merits as a human being.

To apply any other test—to deny a man his hopes because of his color or race, his religion or the place of his birth—is not only to d injustice, it is to deny America and to dishonor the dead who gave their lies for American freedom.

The Right to Vote

Our fathers believed that if this noble view of the rights of man was to flourish, it must be rooted in democracy. The most basic right of all was the right to choose your own leaders. The history of this country, in large measure, is the history of the expansion of that right to all of our people.

Many o the issues of civil rights are very complex and most difficult. But about this there can and should be no argument. Every American citizen must have an equal right to vote. There is no reason which can excuse the denial of that right. There is no duty which weighs more heavily on us than the duty we have to ensure that right.

Yet the harsh fact is that in many places in this country men and women are kept from voting simply because they are Negroes.

Every device of which human ingenuity is capable has been used to deny this right. The Negro citizen may go to register only to be told that the day is wrong, or the hour is late, or the official in charge is absent. And if he persists, and if he manages to present himself to the registrar, he may be disqualified because he did not spell out his middle name or because he abbreviated a word on the application.

And if he manages to fill out an application he is given a test. The registrar is the sole judge of whether he passes this test. He may be asked to recite the entire Constitution, or explain the most complex provisions of State law. And even a college degree cannot be used to prove that he can read and write.

For the fact is that the only way to pass these barriers is to show a white skin.

Experience has clearly shown that the existing process of law cannot overcome systematic and ingenious discrimination. No law that we now have on the books—

and I have helped to put three of them there—can ensure the right to vote when local officials are determined to deny it.

In such a case our duty must be clear to all of us. The Constitution says that no person shall be kept from voting because of his race or his color. We have all sworn an oath before God to support and to defend that Constitution. We must now act in obedience to that oath.

Guaranteeing the Right to Vote

Wednesday I will send to Congress a law designed to eliminate illegal barriers to the right to vote.

The broad principles of that bill will be in the hands of the Democratic and Republican leaders tomorrow. After they have reviewed it, it will come here formally as a bill. I am grateful for this opportunity to come here tonight at the invitation of the leadership to reason with my friends, to give them my views, and to visit with my former colleagues.

I have had prepared a more comprehensive analysis of the legislation which I had intended to transmit to the clerk tomorrow but which I will submit to the clerks tonight. But I want to really discuss with you now briefly the main proposals of this legislation.

This bill will strike down restrictions to voting in all elections—Federal, State, and local—which have been used to deny Negroes the right to vote.

This bill will establish a simple, uniform standard which cannot be used, however ingenious the effort, to flout our Constitution.

It will provide for citizens to be registered by officials of the United States Government if the State officials refuse to register them.

It will eliminate tedious, unnecessary lawsuits which delay the right to vote. Finally, this legislation will ensure that property registered individuals are not prohibited from voting.

I will welcome the suggestions from all the Members of Congress—I have no doubt that I will get some—on ways and means to strengthen this law and to make it effective. But experience has plainly shown that this is the only path to carry out the command of the Constitution.

To those who seek to avoid action by their National Government in their own communities; who want to and who seek to maintain purely local control over elections, the answer is simple:

THE POSSUM HUNTER

Open your polling places to all your people.
Allow men and women to register and vote whatever the color of their skin.
Extend the rights of citizenship to every citizen of this land.
The Need for Action
There is no constitutional issue here. The command of the Constitution is plain.
There is no moral issue. It is wrong—deadly wrong—to deny any of your fellow Americans the right to vote in this country.
There is no issue of States rights or national rights. There is only the struggle for human rights.
I have not the slightest doubt what will be your answer.
The last time a President sent a civil rights bill to the Congress it contained a provision to protect voting rights in Federal elections. That civil rights bill was passed after 8 long months of debate. And when that bill came to my desk from the Congress for my signature, the heart of the voting provision had been eliminated.
This time, on this issue, there must be no delay, no hesitation and no compromise with our purpose.
We cannot, we must not, refuse to protect the right of every American to vote in every election that he may desire to participate in.
And we ought not and we cannot and we must not wait another 8 months before we get a bill. We have already waited a hundred years and more, and the time for waiting is gone.
So I ask you to join me in working long hours—nights and weekends, if necessary—to pass this bill. And I don't make that request lightly. For from the window where I sit with the problems of our country I recognize that outside this chamber is the outraged conscience of a nation, the grave concern of many nations, and the harsh judgment of history on our acts.

We Shall Overcome
But even if we pass this bill, the battle will not be over. What happened in Selma is part of a far larger movement which reaches into every section and State of America. It is the effort of American Negroes to secure for themselves the full blessings of American life.
Their cause must be our cause too. Because it is not just Negroes but really it is all of us, who must overcome the crippling legacy of bigotry and injustice.
And we shall overcome.

S. EARL WILSON, III

As a man whose roots go deeply into Southern soil I know how agonizing racial feelings are. I know how difficult it is to reshape the attitudes and the structure of our society.

But a century has passed, more than a hundred years, since the Negro was freed. And he is not fully free tonight.

It was more than a hundred years ago that Abraham Lincoln, a great President of another party, signed the Emancipation Proclamation, but emancipation is a proclamation and not a fact.

A century has passed, more than a hundred years, since equality was promised. And yet the Negro is not equal.

A century has passed since the day of promise. And the promise is unkept.

The time of justice has now come. I tell you that I believe sincerely that no force can hold it back. It is right in the eyes of man and God that it should come. And when it does, I think that day will brighten the lives of every American.

For Negroes are not the only victims. How many white children have gone uneducated, how many white families have lived in stark poverty, how many white lives have been scarred by fear, because we have wasted our energy and our substance to maintain the barriers of hatred and terror?

So I say to all of you here, and to all in the Nation tonight, that those who appeal to you to hold on to the past do so at the cost of denying you your future.

This great, rich, restless country can offer opportunity and education and hope to all: black and white, North and South, sharecropper and city dweller. These are the enemies: poverty, ignorance, disease. They are the enemies and not our fellow man, not our neighbor. And these enemies too, poverty, disease and ignorance, we shall overcome.

An American Problem

Now let none of us in any sections look with prideful righteousness on the troubles in another section, or on the problems of our neighbors. There is really no part of America where the promise of equality has been fully kept. In Buffalo as well as in Birmingham, in Philadelphia as well as in Selma, Americans are struggling for the fruits of freedom.

This is one Nation. What happens in Selma or in Cincinnati is a matter of legitimate concern to every American. But let each of us look within our own hearts and our own communities, and let each of us put our shoulder to the wheel to root out injustice wherever it exists.

THE POSSUM HUNTER

As we meet here in this peaceful, historic chamber tonight, men from the South, some of whom wee at Iwo Jima, men from the North who have carried Old Glory to far corners of the world and brought it back without a stain on it, men from the East and from the West, are all fighting together without regard to religion, or color, or region, in Viet Nam. Men from every region fought for us across the world 20 years ago.

And in these common dangers and these common sacrifices the South made its contribution of honor and gallantry no less than any other region of the great Republic—and in some instances, a great many of them, more.

And I have not the slightest doubt that good men from everywhere in this country, from the Great Lakes to the Gulf of Mexico, from the Golden Gate to the harbors along the Atlantic, will rally together now in this cause to vindicate the freedom of all Americans. For all of us owe this duty; and I believe that all of us will respond to it.

Your President makes that request of every American.

Progress Through the Democratic Process

The real hero of this struggle is the American Negro. His actions and protests, his courage to risk safety and even to risk his life, have awakened the conscience of this Nation. His demonstrations have been designed to call attention to injustice, designed to provoke change, designed to stir reform.

He has called upon us to make good the promise of America. And who among us can say that we would have made the same progress were it not for his persistent bravery, and his faith in American democracy.

For at the real heart of battle for equality is a deep-seated belief in the democratic process. Equality depends not on the force of arms or tear gas but upon the force of moral right, not on recourse to violence but on respect for law and order.

There have been many pressures upon your President and there will be others as the days come and go. But I pledge you tonight that we intend to fight this battle where it should be fought: in the courts, and in the Congress, and in the hearts of men.

We must preserve the right of free speech and the right of free assembly. But the right of free speech does not carry with it, as has been said, the right to holler fire in a crowded theater. We must preserve the right to free assembly, but free assembly does not carry with it the right to block public thoroughfares to traffic.

S. EARL WILSON, III

We do have a right to protest, and a right to march under conditions that do not infringe the constitutional rights of our neighbors. And I intend to protect all those rights as long as I am permitted to serve in this office.

We will guard against violence, knowing it strikes from our hands the very weapons which we seek—progress, obedience to law, and belief in American values.

In Selma as elsewhere we seek and pray for peace. We seek order. We seek unity. But we will not accept the peace of stifled rights, or the order imposed by fear, or the unity that stifles protest. For peace cannot be purchased at the cost of liberty.

In Selma tonight, as in every—and we had a good day there—as in every city, we are working for just and peaceful settlement. We must all remember that after this speech I am making tonight, after the police and the FBI and the Marshals have all gone, and after you have promptly passed this bill, the people of Selma and the other cities of the Nation must still live and work together. And when the attention of the Nation has gone elsewhere they must try to heal the wounds and to build a new community.

This cannot be easily done on a battleground of violence, as the history of the South itself shows. It is in recognition of this that men of both races have shown such an outstandingly impressive responsibility in recent days—last Tuesday, again today.

Rights Must Be Opportunities

The bill that I am presenting to you will be known as a civil rights bill. But, in a larger sense, most of the program I am recommending is a civil rights program. Its object is to open the city of hope to all people of all races.

Because all Americans just must have the right to vote. And we are going to give them that right.

All Americans must have the privileges of citizenship regardless of race. And they are going to have those privileges of citizenship regardless of race.

But I would like to caution you and remind you that to exercise these privileges takes much more than just legal right. It requires a trained mind and a healthy body. It requires a decent home, and the chance to find a job, and the opportunity to escape from the clutches of poverty.

Of course, people cannot contribute to the Nation if they are never taught to read or write, if their bodies are stunted from hunger, if their sickness goes untended, if their life is spent in hopeless poverty just drawing a welfare check.

So we want to open the gates to opportunity. But we are also going to give all our people, black and white, the help that they need to walk through those gates.

THE POSSUM HUNTER

The Purpose of the Government
My first job after college was as a teacher in Cotulla, Texas, in a small Mexican-American school. Few of them could speak English, and I couldn't speak much Spanish. My students were poor and they often came to class without breakfast, hungry. They knew even in their youth the pain of prejudice. They never seemed to know why people disliked them. But they knew it was so, because I saw it in their eyes. I often walked home late in the afternoon, after the classes were finished, wishing there was more that I could do. But all I knew was to teach them the little that I knew, hoping that it might help them against the hardships that lay ahead.

Somehow you never forget what poverty and hatred can do when you see its scars on the hopeful face of a young child.

I never thought then, in 1928, that I would be standing here in 1965. It never even occurred to me in my fondest dreams that I might have the chance to help the sons and daughters of those students and to help people like them all over this country.

But now I do have that chance—and I'll let you in on a secret—I mean to use it. And I hope that you will use it with me.

This is the richest and most powerful country which ever occupied the globe. The might of past empires is little compared to ours. But I do not want to be the President who built empires, or sought grandeur, or extended dominion.

I want to be the President who educated young children to the wonders of their world. I want to be the President who helped to feed the hungry and to prepare them to be taxpayers instead of taxeaters.

I want to be the President who helped the poor to find their own way and who protected the right of every citizen to vote n every election.

I want to be the President who helped to end hatred among his fellow men and who promoted love among the people of all races and all regions and all parties.

I want to be the President who helped to end war among the brothers of this earth.

And so at the request of your beloved Speaker and the Senator from Montana; the majority leader, the Senator from Illinois; the minority leader, Mr. McCulloch, and other Members of both parties, I came here tonight—not as President Roosevelt came down one time in person to veto a bonus bill, not as President Truman came down one time to urge the passage of a railroad bill—but I came down here to ask you to share this task with me and to share it with the people that we both work for. I want

S. EARL WILSON, III

this to be the Congress, Republicans and Democrats alike, which did all these things for all these people.

Beyond this great chamber, out yonder in 50 States, are the people that we serve. Who can tell what deep and unspoken hopes are in their hearts tonight as they sit there and listen. We all can guess, from our own lives, how difficult they often find their own pursuit of happiness, how many problems each little family has. They look most of all to themselves for their futures. But I think that they also look to each of us.

Above the pyramid on the great seal of the United States it says—in Latin—"God has favored our undertaking."

God will not favor everything that we do. It is rather our duty to divine His will. But I cannot help believing that He truly understands and that He really favors the undertaking

This speech gave Mordecai new faith and new hope to believe again that the future of the black people in America would not be denuded, unpromising or bleak. That the insults, punches, knocks, and kicks that he endured for freedom's sake were not in vain. This man spoke with a Southern drawl, not with a Yankee accent!

JANUARY 1965—THIRD YEAR OF COLLEGE

Tougaloo College has an exchange student program with Brown University in Providence, Rhode Island. Fannie Mae was selected to study at Brown for the fall/winter semester in mathematics. She had never been this far away from home before but felt no apprehension. She adjusted well. Tougaloo had provided her money for the winter clothings she would need. She didn't know anybody outside the exchange program people, and she definitely was not an adventurer. Therefore, she devoted most of her time to studying. All of her professors were brilliant with doctoral degrees from Brown itself, MIT, Harvard, Princeton, and Stanford. For the first time in her life, she had to struggle to make "As" but with her constant studying, questioning the professors, even going to them for help in understanding, she prevailed.

Her teachers loved her eagerness to learn and understand. Her professor of Infinitesimal Calculus and Non-Euclidean Geometry was the only man of color she came across. She loved him. He was brilliant, kind and patient. He would explain over and over again until she understood. He was a young man, perhaps in his late twenties, 28 or 29. He had finished Morehouse College in Atlanta, Georgia with a dual degree in mathematics and physics with a minor in chemistry at the age of 19. From there to MIT for a Master's, then on to Harvard for his doctorate in math at 23 years of age. Dr. Calvin Lucas, III was originally from Birmingham, Alabama, so he could relate to southern black people and he understood the plight of the Negro in Dixie.

S. EARL WILSON, III

One evening after extra help, Fannie Mae and Dr. Lucas were extremely hungry so he invited her to go with him and her Advanced Calculus teacher, a female instructor—Dr. Loren Hunter, Ph.D., Stanford University—to Newport, Rhode Island to relax and grab a bite to eat. She accepted. This would be only her second trip away from the campus since her arrival in January. Her first was an escorted tour to the mall to purchase some winter clothings. In all her life, she had never witnessed a winter as severe as a New England winter. It made Mississippi's winters seem like Sunday school picnics, but being properly dressed, she adjusted and survived. Her reasoning, "If all of these millions of people can endure it, so can I."

Their 32 mile drive from Providence to Newport was to relax themselves and to procure food to ease their hunger symptoms, along with exposing Fannie Mae to other parts of the beautiful state of Rhode Island. She was indeed fascinated with the state's beauty, its waterways like the Narragansett Bay, Rhode Island Sound, and the beautiful gigantic Atlantic Ocean, the likes of which she had never seen before. The largest body of water that she had ever seen was the Ross Barnett Reservoir in Jackson, Mississippi. They were going to a restaurant/bar called The Black Pearl.

The Black Pearl is located along the waters where ships, boats and yachts dock. Some of them are so incredibly beautiful that one could spend hours watching them alone. Most of their wealthy owners take great pride in their uniqueness and beauty and gladly engage you in conversations about them, often inviting one aboard and giving a tour and a drink, a beer, or a glass of wine to boot. Some had brought their servants with them—butlers, cooks, and maids. Some sailed there from other states like Florida, Mississippi, Virginia, Alabama, and Georgia. Very wealthy southerners who stayed autumn through winter to enjoy the New England foliage and winter skiing and snowmobiling and seafood.

There at the Black Pearl the three ate lobsters, clam chowder (Fannie's first), and quahogs, also her first. When asked if she wanted a drink, she replied, "Jack Daniels and Coke, please." This surprised both of her hosts and they ordered the same instead of their usual martinis.

THE POSSUM HUNTER

Professor Loren Hunter's good looks and figure attracted a young Naval officer, graduate of the Naval Academy at Annapolis, about her age (32), and began drinking and dancing with him. You see, in Newport there is a naval base with hundreds of seamen stationed there. When Loren decided to let the officer and gentleman drive her home, Calvin was not too cool with this because he felt concerned about her safety with a stranger. He objected but after her plea, he demanded to see all of the officer's credentials including his driver's license. Another thing that he was not too cool about was being left alone at night with a female student. He cautioned both of them that professors should not appear to, nor date students and that he would never take them out together again. The females only smiled. They both wanted to be alone with the males that they were attracted to.

Dr. Calvin Lucas drove Fannie Mae back to her dormitory. He parked, kissed her, and told her never again. She smiled, thanked him for a good meal, drinks and a lovely night. She explained to him that she did not want to become intimate with him because she wanted to learn and use her brains only, not her body to influence him. He agreed.

At the end of the semester she made four "A+s" using her brains only. When she got her grades she went immediately to Calvin Lucas and said, "I will not thank you for my grades, because I earned them with you helping me to think and learn. For your patience and help I say mucho gracias."

"You are very much welcome, and I feel very proud of you and your accomplishments. One day you will earn your doctorate in mathematics."

He shook her hand. She kissed him and asked, "May I now take you out to dinner? I've given you my brains, now I want to give you my body with no strings attached."

It was an offer Dr. Calvin Lucas could not refuse. Fred and Mordecai would never know, she thought.

Perhaps it had something to do with the way she was dressed, somewhat provocative, but it was the new style she had been introduced to for the younger set in the sixties.

S. EARL WILSON, III

In 1966, Mary Quant, a designer of London, England, produced short waist skimming miniskirts that were about six to seven inches above the knee. Although Mary Quant did not invent the miniskirt, she copied the idea from the designs by Courreges and made them even shorter. It was a daring gamble that the younger (some older) accepted and flaunted from London to America.

It was the day that stockings died and tights were born. It was difficult to wear a miniskirt along with stockings and feel at ease. With tights, there was protection from the weather and no ugly stocking tops, no need for girdles, roll ons and garter belts.

Fannie Mae possessed incredible, beautiful legs and thighs and the wearing of a miniskirt accentuated both. Seeing her in a red, black, tan and white printed surplice bodice skirt with high heel shoes with no stockings whatsoever would make a clergyman stare and a professor cry unless they both were gay

They rode again to the city of Newport, a gem in the Northeast. Fannie Mae sat as close to Calvin as was possible without interfering with his driving while caressing his penis and resting her head on his shoulder. With her first touch, Calvin nearly lost control of the vehicle and gently said to her, "Please don't. I wish to remain alive to really explore your body and to make love to you. Your touching could cause us to have an accident." Fannie smiled and removed her hand. She was well acquainted with the power of her touch. She had plenty of experiences with Mordecai and Fred.

Dr. Calvin Lucas, the connoisseur of fine foods in the New England provinces, chose another restaurant this time. He chose a wondrous place called "The Marring," located on the waterfront. First they parked the car in the Marring's own private parking lot and then walked hand-in-hand to the most beauteous place of dining that Fannie Mae had ever seen. While walking to the restaurant, they passed by sailboats and yachts from all across the United States and some foreign countries. They were things of beauty and joys forever, it seemed, to their owners. No two were exactly alike as though they were personally designed. One of the most intriguing, astonishing aspects was the sun setting over the Newport harbor where the radiant orange light of the sun seemed to

THE POSSUM HUNTER

nestle in the crevices of the water, giving it breathtaking beauty and splendor cascading into the sea. This happens each day but for one, like Fannie, who is seeing it for the very first time is shaken to believe that this is a phenomenon that happened just now.

This can be seen as one dines inside or outside the Marring. As one enters the door, the glorious bar is located on the left where fastidiously dressed bartenders wearing formal shirts, cummerbunds, and black bow ties mix drinks that are to beautiful to drink. These concoctions should be admired and photographed instead of being drunk, like the margaritas Calvin had ordered for them. Passing the reception desk in the middle lies the first dining room with white table cloths with white cloth napkins and superb silverware on top, including the salt and pepper shakers along with silver sugar spoons and bowls and creamers. The lower dining area below is located on, or just above, the water level with the same amenities, plus the invigorating smell and cool breeze exhilarating off the Rhode Island sound. Fannie and Calvin chose to dine at the latter and gaze at the beautiful enchanting sunset. Indeed!

Calvin took full control in ordering the food and drinks. He had no intention of letting Fannie Mae "foot the bill." Although the menu contained steaks, chicken, and chops, he chose New England clam chowder, lobsters, and swordfish steaks with asparagus and potatoes along with French bread. If Fannie Mae disapproved, she showed no remorse between bites.

After a shot of Grand Triple Orange Marnier and a scoop of chocolate soufflé, Fannie Mae excused herself to go to the ladies room where she found their waitress along the way, paid the bill, urinated, and returned to the table. Calvin was hurt but was allowed to pay the tip. He would try to make amends, and he did.

Calvin chose the Hotel Viking to serve as the place for their escapade. Fannie was indeed impressed. The Hotel Viking is located in the heart of Newport's historic Hill District, an elegant haven amid the graceful mansions of Bellevue Avenue off Old Beach Road on Mill Street. The room had only one very large bed covered with a beautiful spread, triple sheets, pillow top mattress, and down pillows. The furniture was Queen Ann style with historic charm and modern amenities like coffee makers and a television. It was reminiscent of the great Newport estates with early 20th century portraits adorning the wall and warm color palate windows covered with luxurious toile. The beveled glass door led into the bathroom's large shower.

Calvin undressed Fannie Mae, and she undressed Calvin. They lay naked in bed together and made passionate unprotected love. This innocent act by two very smart and intelligent single, unmarried people would have drastic bearings on their lives in the future.

The next morning they arose, took a shower, dressed, had breakfast at I-Hop, and returned to Providence. Fannie Mae finished packing and took the railroad train back home that evening. Her thoughts were on this love affair if one could call it that. Certainly there was passion but was there any love? She knew the danger of unprotected sex and the consequences of becoming pregnant but wouldn't it be an honor to have a baby by a man of such intelligence/? With her genes combining with his, the offspring would have to be brilliant indeed. It would be four years before they would meet again.

THE RETURN HOME

The train ride from New York City to Hattiesburg, MS was both refreshing and exhilarating to one who had never before ridden a train. Fannie Mae and another student were driven to Providence, RI from Jackson, MS in the school's station wagon that returned to Tougaloo with two students from Brown University. Both schools conceded that an automobile ride to and from New York's Central Station was more convenient for drivers and students as well.

Fannie had heard about the conditions of train traveling for blacks in the South prior to Martin Luther King's time. Black people who boarded the trains in the southern states were forced to ride in the front cars directly behind the engine. During the days of coal fire and smoke engines, the soot gases sometimes got in the next car carrying the people of color as though they were not already black enough.

Most black folks brought a shoe box filled with food so as not to have to sit at the corner table behind a curtain labeled "for colored only." If that table was filled, blacks would have to stand in line until space became available, no matter if the white section had empty spaces. Even the black waiters were not very courteous to them at times. They considered them country bumpkins. The shoe boxes were their salvations. They were filled with hard-boiled eggs, light bread, fried chicken, mayo and salt mixed with black pepper wrapped in cellophane paper, slices of pound cake, along with tea cakes or cookies. Some people brought ice containers with drinks inside (Cokes, Pepsis, Orange Crush, or Grapettes). Others drank water or purchased drinks from the vendors. Some bought plain drinks, bottles or cans, then purchased ice and cups from the porters.

It was now 1965. Segregation on trains and buses had been abolished, and Fannie Mae and other colored folks could ride and eat anywhere they chose. Although she sat at the middle table, ordered and ate lamb chops, her thoughts went back to opossum and coon. The old saying prevails, "You can take a nig out of the country, but you can't take the country out of the nig."

ARRIVAL AT THE HATTIESBURG DEPOT

Fred Woullard drove from Jackson to Hattiesburg to pick her up in his Volkswagen. She unboarded. They hugged, kissed, then placed her luggage under the front hood of his vehicle, then started the journey back to Tougaloo. "Will you please take me to my house before we head to Jackson?" she asked Fred. "I want to see my family."
"Of course. I would like to meet my future in-laws," said Fred.
They drove to the country, into the woods. Fred became bewildered by the absence of anything except trees, dirt roads, bushes, birds, and insects. Occasionally they passed houses in between long drives from each other where people always smiled and waved their hands. Some even yelled and hollered, "How ya'll doing?" Fred was admixed. How could people live this far apart? He had been to Central Park in New York but it was most of the time filled with people, singing, dancing, running, jogging, skating, playing ball, eating, drinking, couples holding hands and walking. Here there was nothing. How weird!
An opossum ran in their direction in front of the car and was hit by the car. Fred cried, "Oh, no! What have I done?"
"Stop, stop!" said Fannie Mae. She got out of the car, lifted the dead creature by its tail, and placed it on the floor of the vehicle.
Fred was devastated. "What have I done?" he cried. "What the hell is that?"
"It's an epicurean dish that people around here eat. It's an opossum."
"Shouldn't we dig a hole and bury it?" he asked.
"No, sir-eee," said Fannie. "This is lunch."

S. EARL WILSON, III

When they drove into her yard, there was her father Thomas, mother Ester Lee, her sister Mae Helen and Lonzo, her brother. "Well, look who done come home," said Thomas. "Did the dog drag you in?" "Welcome, light and look at your saddle."

Sensing Fred's confusion, Fannie whispered to him, "That's the country folks' way of saying, 'Welcome, come on in.' In the olden days, people used to visit each other by riding their horses with saddles. To light means to get down from your horse. As the host would lead your horse away, you were asked to look at your saddle, then relax and enjoy the food or refreshments."

"Oh," said Fred, "I reckon I will, but don't feed me any possum." They smiled.

They had a jolly good time eating biscuits, fried chicken with greens, rice and gravy. Lonzo took Fred around to the back of the house where he showed him their pet raccoon which astounded him. "Beautiful but ugly at the same time!" exclaimed Fred.

The fire was built. The embers were hot so the cleansing and cooking of the opossum began. Fred was enthralled by the whole procedure of throwing the creature into the hot burning embers removing its hair, boiling it in salty water, seasoning it and baking it in an oven. When given a piece of it to taste he almost regurgitated but held on to his composure. "Not bad," he lied as he took his first bite and swallowed. No, it didn't taste like Nathan's hot dogs on Coney Island.

Because of Fannie's excellent representation of Tougaloo at Brown making all A's, she was asked to teach a course in math to incoming freshmen that summer. The pay was good—$500.00, plus room and board. Mordecai was there repeating a course in trigonometry where he would solicit Fannie's help. They were still friends. Both Fred and Bessie Mae knew and gave their approvals. Love can end but friendship remains between country home folks. They were both confident of their hold on their loved ones and their lovemaking techniques.

Around the second week of summer school, Fannie became concerned about her menstrual cycle. It hadn't come. Could she be pregnant? If so, who would the father be, Fred Woullard or Dr. Calvin Lucas? She was smart enough to make "A's" in all her subjects but not smart enough to have unprotected sex. She was so grateful and eager to have sex with Dr. Lucas that she forgot to instruct him to us prophylactics, which he didn't. Two geniuses performing a dumb act.

When she and Fred left her family's house, she directed him to a secluded area that she and Mordecai had used over and over again to make love. There really was no need to hide because they were already in the woods with nothing but trees. As the Ink Spots used to sing—"I talk to the trees but they won't listen to me." There were no thoughts of precaution. Mother Nature ruled! How thrilling to make love in the open without the worry of being seen, with grass, land, flowers, running brooks, trees and harmless wildlife as your only company.

Fannie waited two more weeks, still no flow. She told Fred, and he hit the panic button. "We are both honor students with bright futures ahead of us. You can be a candidate for a doctoral degree in mathematics from great universities. I have already been assured entrance to Johns Hopkin University's Medical School," Fred said. "Let's be sure and see a doctor out of town. Let's visit a white doctor so no word will get out," he said.

"But what if it's true?" Fannie asked Fred.

"Let's find out first before we make any rational decisions. If you really are pregnant, then it is early. Perhaps we can have an abortion." This was like driving a stake through Fannie's heart. Abortion was the last thing she wanted. Her religion taught her that abortion is murder. Her logic told her that it could be the child of a brilliant man and a brilliant woman. This child could be born brilliant and perhaps discover, invent, or create things that would benefit mankind. No, her baby had to be born and she had to marry so that their names would not be scandalized.

Fannie and Fred drove to Canton, Mississippi to see a white doctor whose waiting rooms were still segregated. "Good," thought Fred. Since the civil rights movement, no blacks would come to a segregated doctor.

They took Fannie away to the "colored" examination room to test her for pregnancy. The results were positive, and they both cried. Fred could see his career drifting away to a girl who ate possums. "What a waste!" he cried.

Fannie did not comprehend what he meant. "We will have to get married," Fannie said. "I won't have an abortion."

"We'll see," said Fred. "We'll talk about it tomorrow evening. Ok?"

"Ok," she said.

They drove in silence all the way back from Canton to Tougaloo. The only sound was that of the Volkswagen's motor and Fannie's crying.

That very night, Fred Woullard packed his Volkswagen with all of his belongings and headed back to New York. He wrote Fannie a letter and gave it to Mordecai to deliver to her. Mordecai agreed to do so without questions. Fred's time in Mississippi was now over. He would complete his mission at Columbia, as a bachelor, who would get his bachelor's degree with honors.

Everybody, it seemed, knew about Fred Woullard's departure except Fannie Mae, even Mordecai. Mordecai called Fannie Mae on the phone and asked that she meet him at Judson Cross Hall's entrance way. She agreed. Fannie was there waiting when Mordecai arrived.

"Hello, Fannie."

"Hello, Mordecai."

"Let's take a walk if it's alright with you."

"It's alright."

As they walked, Mordecai said, "Fred Woullard has packed his car and left campus."

"Oh, no! He what?"

"Left campus last night with all of his possessions." After having to repeat freshman English twice, Mordecai had learned to talk much better.

"That lowdown dirty S.O.B. ran away from me like a scalded hog. What am I gonna do?" she cried, with her face filled with tears.

"He asked me to give you this." He handed the letter to Fannie Mae. She opened it and read:

"My Innocent Love,

THE POSSUM HUNTER

Darling Fannie, I truly do love and adore you without limits. I love you more today than yesterday and really intended for you to be my mate for the rest of my life but I cannot marry you now. It would upset my life that I have dedicated to others. I must succeed in becoming a doctor.

You see, I come from a family of five, a mother who lost her husband, my father when I was sixteen years of age. My father was a high school dropout from Bessemer, Alabama that lost his job at the steel mill, then moved to New York seeking his fortune. Because of his lack of education the best job that he could find was that of a truck driver/ delivery man for clothing stores in the city. My mother, from Birmingham, too quit school in the 11th grade to follow my father. She works at a garment factor in Chinatown in New York. From their marriage three children were produced, all with good minds and the promise of achieving educational goals that their parents never reached.

Their oldest child, my brother Al, got to the twelfth grade, then quit to sell drugs. He lost his life in a police drug raid when he refused to surrender his pistol. He was shot twice in the chest. This devastated our family, and still there was no high school diploma in our family. The second oldest, my beautiful sister Grace, had an IQ of 140 and straight "A's" into her senior year at Girl's High School in New York. She became pregnant the middle of her senior year, dropped out of school and married a cocaine addict who is now in prison. She and her baby returned home.

I am the youngest child and our family's only hope who not only finished high school as valedictorian but attends Tougaloo College as one of their honor students. I cannot help but to succeed. I owe it to my mother, my deceased father and brother, my sister and her child, my grandparents on both sides of my family in Alabama. Already they have boasted about their future doctor in the family.

I beg you to forgive me. God bless you and the baby.

With never-ending love I remain yours forever, Fred"

"Mordecai, I'm pregnant with Fred's or maybe somebody else's baby. I wanted and hoped that Fred would save my honor by marrying me. Now he's gone. I'm going to be scandalized both here at Tougaloo and back home." Then tears flowed from her eyes like water from a leaking faucet. Her body shook as though she were having an epileptic fit. She was devastated indeed.

"Oh, Mordecai, what will become of me? My name will be scandalized and my baby will have no father to care for him or name to carry. Why did I ever leave Hungerville only to return in disgrace? Oh, Mordecai, why did we ever break up?"

Mordecai held Fannie Mae in his arms. He began to reminisce about their olden days and wiped her tears away. He thought about how they used to love each other, how their relationship grew, brought them together at Tougaloo, then faded into oblivion. He held her tenderly and kissed her cheeks.

"Mordecai, marry me, please, and give my child your name and keep me from being scandalized. Stay with me for awhile, then I'll give you your freedom."

"All right, Fannie Mae, I'll marry you, but I can't stay or live with you and another man's baby. We'll marry and save you and the baby's name. Then I'll join the Army and go away to Vietnam for a while. I need time away to think anyway. I'll probably fail trig again with you not being here, and Bessie Mae is fooling around on me with Dr. Hodges. I caught her coming from his apartment last week. She said they didn't do nothing, and she let him feel her legs, and he is going to give both of us "A's" but I don't want no woman who let teachers feel over her body. I also think that she is going with Bubber Smith. I just don't trust her anymore. I need time away time to think and make up my mind."

The very next day Mordecai went into Jackson and volunteered to serve his country as a United States Marine. He was given three days to report for induction. Remarkably, he passed all tests with flying colors. That day was Friday. He had until 12:00 Monday to report.

That Sunday he and Fannie Mae were married on Tougaloo's campus in the Woodworth Chapel. This was the most exciting and talked about event on campus the entire summer.

No one knew that she was pregnant, so the bride wore white, and the groom wore a black suit. Her bridesmaids were all members of her sorority, and the best man was his fraternity brother. Her mom and dad

THE POSSUM HUNTER

plus Alonzo rode the Greyhound bus to Jackson along with Mordecai's family.

It was a beautiful wedding with the bridesmaids dressed in their scintillating sorority colors of red and white and the groom's fraternity brothers adorning their ornaments of purple and gold. Both the bride and groom cried. Such a paradox—her tears were tears of relief while his tears were tears of grief, even though he was saving the honor of someone he had once loved dearly and intended to marry. His mind drifted back to the very first time they went coon hunting together when they both fell in love with each other. He thought about the night she shed him of his virginity. It was charming, delightful, ecstatic, and erotic!

Fannie Mae was indeed an alluring and beautiful bride and had she not been caring the fetus of someone else, Mordecai would have been honored to be the groom. However, jealousy and sadness gripped his bowels, and he could not eliminate them.

Mordecai was both admixed and perplexed. Perhaps he still loved her? He didn't know. Could there have been a resurgence of love?

Fannie Mae would conceal her abdomen and suppress it with corsets all summer and continued to teach till the summer school's end. She would not return to Tougaloo the ensuing fall. All of her dreams and aspirations were now blown into the winds of regret. She questioned how God could give her such a beautiful mind good enough to calculate numbers, comprehend facts, analyze formulas, understand the abstract, to formulate and construct ideas, and yet, a mind so stupid as to allow her to succumb to sexual temptations that would destroy her future. A "bedswerver"? (Shakespeare)

She thought of Dr. Martin Luther King, Jr.'s words: *We must remember that intelligence is not enough. Intelligence plus character—that is the goal of true education.* Fannie Mae believed that she had fallen short of the goal. This was her retribution.

It was now approximately one month after Fannie Mae's sexual interludes. She and her husband Modechai made love over and over again the night of their wedding in a modern Holiday Inn in Jackson, Mississippi. This was the same one that Gizelle Junaita Haniford had taken him to. Modechai felt a touch of guiltiness but suppressed it with the thought of Fannie's sins. Perhaps he could forgive her but tomorrow he would be gone.

Mordecai was sent to Washington, D.C. on the Southern Railroad from Hattiesburg, Mississippi by the United States Marine Corps. His destination for the beginning of his basic training would be at Quantico Marine Corps Base in Quantico, Virginia, 35 miles south of Washington, D.C. This was a vast area of over 100 square miles and the top Marine military base in the world. In addition to military training and duty, there were an FBI facility, a museum, and other important buildings of national concerns.

By Mordecai being a country boy and in great physical shape, it made the gruesome Marine tactics much easier to master than normal recruits. He adjusted well. He was given a leadership role as squad leader and adjusted well to military life. He already knew how to run with a gun over rugged terrain through the woods, across swampy areas, into fields of vegetation, ponds, creeks, and springs. His searching for a new life away from everybody he knew was a great incentive for him to achieve. Mordecai became a very good soldier. This would be his resilience, his resurgence.

SOUTHEAST ASIA

August 2, 1964, the *USS Maddox* was fired upon by torpedoes in the Gulf of Tonkin. August 4, 1964, the *USS Turner Joy* was reportedly fired upon in the same area. There are rumors that this did not actually occur but this launched to retaliation by the USA. Congress gave President Lyndon Johnson the power to conduct military actions in Southeast Asia without declaring war. This marked the initiation of American ground war in Vietnam. Americans viewed that the Vietnam struggle was a step towards halting the advancement of communism.

In March 1965, 3,500 Marines were deployed to the area, of which Corporal Mordecai Johnson was among. A strong and efficient offensive warrior was he, even though their duty there was a defensive maneuver. By December, 200,000 Marines occupied the area.

The Marines are trained for offensive warfare, not defensive warfare, so in May, ARVN forces suffered heavy losses at the Battle of Binh Gia and were defeated. Mordecai held his own and was promoted in June at the Battle of Dong Xoai. Moral plummeted, desertion rates increased, and the American situation was critical. General William Westmoreland suggested abandoning their defensive rules and to take the offensive role. This they did and the U.S. began to stop losing and began to advance in their "search-and-destroy" missions. Operation Starlite was the first major ground offensive by the U.S. soldiers that proved successful.

When not on an offensive maneuver, Sergeant First Class Mordecai Johnson was a member of an elite group called the Search and Rescue Unit. These selected members were brave, skillfully trained in survival and rescue tactics, overly conditioned, strong enough to carry wounded comrades while running to safety, expert riflemen, excellent users of knives and blades and could kill with their hands and bodies (Ju Jitsu or Kung Fu experts).

Not too far behind enemy lines was an Air Force pilot who had ejected from his plane after it had been hit by enemy ground fire. He had parachuted into a tree and couldn't get down. He also had a broken leg. The signal device he used told the Search and Rescue Unit his position. Mordecai and three other members of his squad set out to rescue this wounded officer before the North Vietnamese found him and killed him. Dodging enemy gunfire, Mordecai meandered between enemy lines just like he meandered when possum hunting. He found the pilot dangling from a tree about ten feet high. There he climbed the tree effortlessly like the times he did in coon hunting. He set up a pulley system, secured a rope around the pilot, then cut him free, gently lowering him to the ground.

He was spotted by the enemy, and they began to advance. As he loaded the wounded pilot on his back and began to flee, the enemy began to fire in his direction. The other squad members of the Search and Rescue Unit began to throw grenades and return fire at the North Vietnamese. This allowed Mordecai time to reach the awaiting helicopter with his victim. Mission accomplished! With his passenger and his squad loaded aboard the helicopter, Mordecai began to climb on board when he felt a sharp tingling pain in his right leg. He had been shot by one of those that they had missed. Another bullet penetrated his buttock. He yelled as he lost consciousness.

In the hospital, the bullet in his buttock was removed and all was well there. But his right leg was so severely damaged that it had to be amputated. First Sergeant Mordecai Johnson was promoted to Master Sergeant, given the Purple Heart and the Distinguished Medal of Honor, but his fighting days as a United States Marine were over.

After six months in the hospital in Germany, he was sent to Walter Reed Hospital in Washington, D.C. to recover and to be taught how to use the prosthetic leg so he could walk again. He was sad, angry, a very poor and difficult patient. He refused to cooperate and began using

THE POSSUM HUNTER

drugs. He hated his wheelchair but preferred it to an artificial limb and foot. His favorite pastime of hunting was over and he cried for his pilgrimage of possum hunting.

His wife Fannie Mae had now given birth to a son she named Willie B. Johnson. They had plenty of money because she had saved most of the allotment money the armed forces provided for her and her child. The hazardous pay for duty in Vietnam plus the extra pay for being a Search and Rescue member came to about $15,000 between them. They were, indeed, the wealthiest black folks in Hungerville, Mississippi.

Fannie Mae was informed of his condition and drove their new Chevy sedan to Washington, D.C. Mordecai refused to see her and the child. He blamed her for the remorseful condition he was in. If she had not gotten pregnant, he would not have had to marry her out of pity, and none of this would have happened.

Three times she tried to see him. Three times he refused. Now remember, Fannie Mae possessed a brilliant mind. The fourth time she secured a nurse's uniform, put it on, and walked unnoticed into his room where he sat smoking a reefer. His back was turned from the door as he gazed out the window watching traffic. She approached his wheelchair silently, then touched him on his shoulder. As he turned to face the unexpected visitor, she planted a sweet, gentle kiss upon his lips, then embraced him awkwardly. He was terrified and happy and angry all at the same time, simultaneously. He didn't want anybody he knew to see him in this condition but cherished the emotion of a kiss. It was now 1966, and he had not kissed anyone since 1964. The Vietnam women that he made love to, he never kissed, only embraced and had sex. When finished, he paid his money and left.

"What made you come here? I wrote you not to come," said Mordecai angrily.

"I came because I'm your wife whether you want me or not. When we took our vows we both said 'in sickness or in health, to death do we part.' You need me. You need somebody to care for you. You are in a rut, and you need to get out of it. They told me about your drug habits, and that's the second thing that you are going to do—break the habit. You are like a possum up a simmon tree that can't get down!"

"Well, what's the first thing that takes precedence over the second?" he asked.

"The first thing you are going to do is make love to me. I haven't made love since our wedding night." She closed the door and the curtains around his bed and guided his wheelchair to his bed. There she straddled his lap, took out his penis, and sat down on it like the first time they had sex in her house. This time Mordecai did shout, and the nurses came running in. Fannie Mae simply stood up and moved away. He covered himself with his hands.

"What's wrong? What's the matter?"

"Nothing," he lied. "I got my finger caught in the wheel of the chair as I moved it. Everything is alright." They smiled and left, then Fannie Mae resumed her position, this time facing him and kissing him. For the both of them it was ecstasy and joy divine. They fell in love again.

Mordecai was checked out of the hospital. His belongings were packed into the trunk and backseat of their Chevy and Fannie began the long drive back to their home in Hungerville, Mississippi, with the baby in Mordecai's lap. There would be no use of drugs or alcohol on this three day journey back home. This would be the beginning of his rehabilitation. Although he suffered and craved marijuana and cocaine, Fannie Mae would not relent to take him to the places that they could be procured. As he cried and begged, his only consolations were prayers, soft drinks, and chewing gum. About 3:00 a.m., they stopped along Highway 98 as Mordecai seemed to be having an epileptic fit. His shaking and sweating and crying only merited her pity and consolation. She wrapped him in a blanket, wiped his face, and prayed. They were in "redneck country" in North Carolina, a place called Creedmore, North Carolina, a few miles north of Durham. Suddenly there appeared a police car with a constable and a deputy, both members of the Caucasian race. With their siren blasting, their lights flickering, they approached the car shining their flashlights in Fannie and Mordecai's faces and uttered these words, "Get out the car, niggers!"

Fannie Mae obeyed but before she could explain, the constable drew his pistol, pointed it and his flashlight into the faces of Mordecai and the boy, and asked, "You hard of hearing, boy? I said get out of the car."

THE POSSUM HUNTER

Mordecai replied, "I can't get out because I only have one leg."

Then the deputy opened the door and there sat Mordecai with only one leg. "How did you lose your other leg? In a car accident driving too fast while you were drunk?"

"No, sir," Mordecai said. "I lost it in Vietnam fighting for my country and people like you."

Both the deputy and the constable felt somewhat ashamed and reduced their speeding fine to $50.00 cash. "Well, why did y'all pull up alongside of the road?"

"I had to pee, and I didn't want to cause any uproar by going to your all white motels."

They let them go. Fannie Mae drove on into Durham, North Carolina where they spent the night with two Tougaloo graduates who lived there and worked for the North Carolina Mutual Life Insurance Company, a black owned cooperation. Fannie stated to Mordecai, "By you not having the ability to walk could have cost both our lives. You must learn to use the limb and how to walk again." Mordecai agreed and promised to try.

Although he was cured of drug use, they thought, they wanted to be certain and sought help. The VFW (Veterans of Foreign Wars) in Hattiesburg referred them to the Veterans Hospital in Jackson, Mississippi for rehabilitation, both in walking and stoppage of drug use. It was Mordecai's decision to rent a cottage big enough for two people and a child near Tougaloo's campus. He had grown to love the child and became attached to him. With his veteran's 100% compensation, his G.I. bill, and shopping privileges at military PX's they both could go back to school at Tougaloo and finish their undergraduate education.

They both reenrolled at Tougaloo and graduated in 1968 a month after Martin Luther King, Jr. was shot to death on the balcony of the Lorraine Motel in Memphis, Tennessee. White former convict James Earl Ray was arrested for his murder, pled guilty, and was sentenced to 99 years in prison.

King, on April 3, 1968, the day before his assassination, gave his now famous *I've Been to the Mountaintop* speech:

"It really doesn't matter what happens now...some began to...talk abut the threats that were out—what would happen to me from some of our sick white brothers...Like anybody, I would like to live a long life. Longevity has its place, but I'm not concerned about that now. I just want to do God's will. And He's allowed me to go up to the mountain! And I've looked over, and I've seen the Promised Land. I may not get there with you. But I want you to know tonight, that we, as a people, will get to the Promised Land. And so I'm happy tonight. I'm not worried about anything. I'm not fearing any man. My eyes have seen the Glory of the coming of the Lord!"

Martin Luther King, Jr.'s room was 306 at the Lorraine Motel, owned by Walter Bailey. This room was so often used by King and his friend Ralph Abernathy that it was referred to as the "King-Abernathy Suite." When King stood on the second floor's balcony, he was shot at 6:01 p.m., April 4, 1968. The bullet struck his right cheek, smashing his jaw and then traveled down his spine and lodged in his shoulder. Martin Luther King, Jr. was declared dead at St. Joseph's Hospital at 7:05 p.m.

This led to riots across America in about 60 cities and resulted in numerous deaths. President Lyndon B. Johnson declared a national day of mourning for "The King." Over 300,000 people attended his funeral which began at Ebenezer Baptist Church. The body was then carried to the campus of his alma mater, Morehouse College in Atlanta, Georgia, where his mentor, Dr. Benjamin E. Mays, President Emeritus of Morehouse College, would deliver the eulogy. They had agreed that if either one of them should die before the other, the living one would eulogize the deceased. On April 9, 1968, Mays made good on the promise.

After funeral services at Ebenezer Baptist Church, King's mahogany coffin was born to Morehouse College on a rickety farm wagon pulled by two mules. There, Mays, the school's 70-year-old president emeritus, delivered a final eulogy that also renounced what many saw coming: a turn toward violence for the black movement. King was "more courageous than those who advocate violence as a way out," Mays told the estimated 150,000 mourners. "Martin Luther King faced the dogs, the police, jail, heavy criticism, and finally death; and he never carried a

THE POSSUM HUNTER

gun, not even a knife to defend himself. He had only his faith in a just God to rely on."

Indeed, King's assassination by James Earl Ray left many questioning the future of nonviolence protest in the late 1960s. Quoted in *Time* magazine a week after King's funeral, Floyd McKissick, chairman of the Congress of Racial Equality, offered this sober judgment: "The way things are today, not even Christ could come back and preach nonviolence."

To be honored by being requested to give the eulogy at the funeral of Dr. Martin Luther King is like asking one to eulogize his deceased son—so close and so precious was he to me. Our friendship goes back to his student days at Morehouse. It is not an easy task; nevertheless I accept with a sad heart and with full knowledge of my inadequacy to do justice to do this man. It was my desire that if I predeceased Dr. King, he would pay tribute to me on my final day. It was his wish that if he predeceased me, I would deliver the homily at his funeral. Fate has

S. EARL WILSON, III

decreed that I eulogize him. I wish it might have been otherwise; for, after all I am years and 10 and Martin Luther is dead at 39.

Although there are some who rejoice in death, there are millions across the length and breadth of this world who are smitten with grief that this friend of mankind—all mankind has been cut down in the flower of his youth. So, multitudes here and in foreign lands: kings, heads of governments, the clergy of the world, and the common man everywhere are praying that God will be with the family, the American people, and the president of the United States in this tragic hour. We hope that this universal concern will bring comfort to the family—for grief is like a heavy load: when shared it is easier to bear. We come today to help the family carry the load.

We have assembled here from every section of this great nation and from other parts of the world to give thanks to God that He gave to America at this moment in history, Martin Luther King, Jr. Truly, God is no respecter of persons. How strange! God called the grandson of a slave on his father's side, and the grandson of a man born during the Civil War on his mother's side, and said to him: Martin Luther, speak to America about war and peace; about social justice and racial discrimination; about its obligations to the poor; and about nonviolence as a way of perfecting social change in a world of brutality and war.

Here was a man who believed with all of his might that the pursuit of violence at any time is ethically and morally wrong; that God and the moral weight of the universe are against it; that violence is self-defeating; and that only love and forgiveness can break the vicious cycle of revenge. He believed that nonviolence would prove effective in the abolition of injustice in politics, in economics, in education, and in race relations. He was convinced, also, that people could not be moved to abolish voluntarily the inhumanity of man to man by mere persuasion and pleading, but that they could be moved to do so by dramatizing the evil through massive nonviolent resistance. He believed that nonviolent direct action was necessary to supplement the nonviolent victories won by federal courts. He believed that the nonviolent approach to solving social problems would ultimately prove to be redemptive.

THE POSSUM HUNTER

Out of this conviction, history records the marches in Montgomery, Birmingham, Selma, Chicago and other cities. He gave people an ethical and moral way to engage in activities designed to perfect social change without bloodshed and violence; and when violence did erupt it was that which is potential in any protest which aims to uproot deeply entrenched wrongs. No reasonable person would deny that the activities and the personality of Martin Luther King, Jr. contributed largely to the success of the student sit-in movements in abolishing segregation in downtown establishments; and that his activities contributed mightily to the passage of the Civil Rights legislation of 1964 and 1965.

Martin Luther King, Jr. believed in a united America. He believed that the walls of separation brought on by legal and de facto segregation, and discrimination based on race and color, could be eradicated. As he said in his Washington Monument address: "I have a dream."

He had faith in his country. He died striving to desegregate and integrate America to the end that this great nation of ours, born in revolution and blood, conceived in liberty and dedicated to the proposition that all men are created free and equal, will truly become the lighthouse of freedom where none will be denied because his skin is black and none favored because his eyes are blue; where our nation will be militarily strong but perpetually at peace; economically secure but just learned but wise; where the poorest—the garbage collectors—will have bread enough and to spare; where no one will be poorly housed; each educated up to his capacity; and where the richest will understand the meaning of empathy. This was his dream, and the end toward which he strove. As he and his followers so often sang: "We shall overcome someday; black and white together."

Let it be thoroughly understood that our deceased brother did not embrace nonviolence out of fear or cowardice. Moral courage was one of his noblest virtues. As Mahatma Gandhi challenged the British Empire without a sword and won, Martin Luther King, Jr. challenged the interracial wrongs of his country without a gun. And he had the faith to believe that he would win the battle for social justice. I make bold to assert that it took more courage for King to practice nonviolence than it took his assassin to fire the fatal shot. The assassin is a coward. He committed his dastardly deed and fled. When Martin Luther disobeyed an unjust law, he accepted the consequences of his actions. He never ran away and he never begged for mercy. He returned to the Birmingham jail to serve his time.

Perhaps he was more courageous than soldiers who fight and die on the battlefield. There is an element of compulsion in their dying. But when Martin Luther faced death again and again, and finally embraced it, there was no external pressure. He was acting on an inner compulsion that him on. More courageous than those who advocate violence as a way out, for they carry weapons of destruction. But Martin Luther faced the dogs, the police, jail, heavy criticism, and finally death; and he never carried a gun, not even a knife to defend himself. He had only his faith in a just God to rely on; and the belief that "thrice is he armed who has his quarrels just." The faith that Browning writes about when he says:

'One who never turned his back but marched breast forward
Never doubted clouds would break
Never dreamed, though right were worsted, wrong would triumph
Held we fall to rise, and to fight better
Sleep to wake.'

Coupled with moral courage was Martin Luther King Jr.'s capacity to love people. Though deeply committed to a program of freedom for Negroes, he had love and concern for all kinds of peoples. He drew no distinction between the high and low; none between the rich and the poor. He believed especially that he was sent to champion the cause of the man farthest down. He would probably that if death had to come, I am sure there was no greater cause to die for than fighting to get a wage for garbage collectors. He was supra-race, supra-nation, supra-denomination, supra-class, supra-culture. He belonged to the world and to mankind. Now he belongs to posterity.

But there is a dichotomy in all this. This man was loved by some and hated by others. If any man knew the meaning of suffering, King knew. House bombed; living day by day for 13 years under constant threats of death; maliciously accused of being a Communist; falsely accused of being insincere and seeking limelight for his own glory; stabbed by a member of his own race; slugged in a hotel lobby; jailed 30 times; occasionally deeply hurt because his friends betrayed him—and yet this man had not bitterness in his heart, no rancor in his soul, no revenge in his mind; and he went up and down the length and breadth of this world preaching nonviolence and the redemptive power of love. He believed with all of his heart, mind and soul that the way to peace and brotherhood is through nonviolence, love and suffering. He was severely criticized for his opposition to the war in Vietnam. It must be said, however, that one could hardly expect a prophet of Dr. King's commitments to advocate nonviolence at home and violence in Vietnam. Nonviolence to King was total commitment not only in solving the problems of race in the United States, but in solving the problems of the world.

Surely this man was called of God to do this work. If Amos and Micah were prophets in the eight century B.C., Martin Luther King Jr. was a prophet in the 20th century. If Isaiah was called of God to prophesy in his day, Martin Luther was called of God to prophesy in his time. If Hosea was sent to preach love and forgiveness centuries ago, Martin Luther was sent to expound the doctrine of nonviolence and forgiveness in the third quarter of the 20th century. If Jesus was called to preach the Gospel to the poor, Martin Luther was called to give dignity to the common man. If a prophet is one who interprets in clear and intelligible language the will of God, Martin Luther King Jr. fits that designation. If a prophet is one who does not seek popular causes to espouse, but rather the cause he thinks are right, Martin Luther qualified on that score.

No! He was not ahead of his time. No man is ahead of his time. Every man is within his star each his time. Each man must respond to the call of God in his lifetime and not in somebody else's. Jesus had to respond to the call of God in the first century A.D. and not in the 20th century. He had but one life to live. He couldn't wait. How long do you think Jesus would have had to wait for constituted authorities to accept him? Twenty-five years? A hundred years? A thousand? He died at 33. He couldn't wait. Paul, Galileo, Copernicus, Martin Luther the Protestant reformer, Gandhi, Nehru couldn't wait for another time.

S. EARL WILSON, III

They had to act in their lifetimes. No man is ahead of his time. Abraham, leaving his country in the obedience to God's call; Moses leading a rebellious people to the Promised Land; Jesus dying on a cross, Galileo on his knees recanting; Lincoln dying of an assassin's bullet; Woodrow Wilson crusading for a League of Nations; Martin Luther King Jr. dying fighting for justice for garbage collectors—none of these men were ahead of their time. With the time was always ripe to do that which was right and that which needed to be done.

Too bad, you say, that Martin Luther King Jr. died so young. I feel that way, too. But, as I have seen many times before, it isn't how long one lives, but how well. It's what one accomplishes for mankind that matters. Jesus died at 33; Joan of Arc at 19; Byron and Burns at 36; Keats at 25; Marlow at 29; Shelley at 30; Dunbar before 35; John Fitzgerald Kennedy at 46; William Rainey Harper at 49; and Martin Luther King Jr. at 39.

We all pray that the assassin will be apprehended and brought to justice. But, make no mistake. The American people are in part responsible for Martin Luther King Jr.'s death. The assassin heard enough condemnation of King and Negroes to feel that he had public support. He knew that millions hated King.

The Memphis officials must bear some of the guilt for Martin Luther's assassination. The strike should have been settled several weeks ago. The lowest paid men in our society should not have to strike for a more just wage. A century after Emancipation, and after the enactment of the 13th and 15th Amendments, it should not have been necessary for Martin Luther King Jr. to stage marches in Montgomery, Birmingham and Selma, and go to jail 30 times trying to achieve for his people those rights which people of lighter hue get by virtue of their being born white. We, too, are guilty of murder. It is time for the American people to repent and make democracy equally applicable to all Americans. What can we do? We, and not the assassin, represent America at its best. We have the power—not the prejudiced, not the assassin—to make things right.

If we love Martin Luther King Jr., and respect him, as this crowd surely testifies, let us see to it he did not die in vain; let us see to it that we do not dishonor his name by trying to solve our problems through rioting in the streets. Violence was foreign to his nature. He warned that continued riots could produce a fascist state. But let us see to it also that the conditions that cause riots promptly removed, as the president of the United States is trying to get us to do so. Let black and white alike search their hearts; and if there be prejudice in our hearts against any racial or ethnic group, let us exterminate it and let us pray, as Martin Luther King Jr. would pray if he could: 'Father, forgive them for they know not what they do.' If we do this, Martin Luther King Jr. will have died a redemptive death from which all mankind will benefit….

I close by saying to you what Martin Luther King Jr. believed: If physical death was the price he had to pay to rid America of prejudice and injustice, nothing could be more redemptive. And to paraphrase the words of the immortal John Fitzgerald Kennedy, permit me to say that Martin Luther King Jr.'s unfinished work on earth must truly be our own. (From *Born to Rebel: An Autobiography by Benjamin E. Mays*. Copyright 1971 by Benjamin Mays. Used by permission of the University of Georgia Press.)

Fannie Mae, Mordecai and his pride, and Professor Dr. Earnest P. Miles all rode together to Atlanta to attend the funeral. This time Dr. Miles' skin color did not merit them any special privileges in obtaining hotel or motel reservations. The city overflowed with people from all across the USA and foreign countries. There were no rooms in the inns! Their only hope of securing a place to rest their weary heads after having driven nonstop from Jackson to Atlanta during the night was a civil rights connection that Mordecai had made during his protesting and marching days. This was at the home of Donald P. Stone, a staunch civil rights activist who lived in Atlanta. Stone was a brilliant chemistry major at Morehouse College who abandoned his sciences after graduation for liberal causes. Although destined for a Ph.D. in chemistry, Stone felt the cause to act for civil rights of black Americans. He was called to duty by another Morehouse activist, Lonnie King. Together they broke many barriers and uplifted freedom for their race. Chemistry took a backseat while civil rights took precedence in Stone's life.

A phone call to Donald did, indeed, get them a sanctuary to stay, although his house was already filed with the likes of Rap Brown, Stokely Carmichael, Attorney Howard Moore and Angela Davis. They stayed with Stone the nights before and after the funeral and departed the next day after a soul food lunch of greens and fried chicken at Pascal's on then called Hunter Street—now renamed Martin Luther King, Jr. Blvd.

Atlanta and the world have made drastic changes since that day. Thousands of those who came returned to make Atlanta their home.

* * * * *

Fannie Mae, after graduating summa cum laude of her class, was overwhelmed with scholarships and offers to further her education at some of America's greatest institutes of higher learning. Offers came from the South: Vanderbilt, Duke, Georgia Tech, LSU, Tulane, Mississippi State, Agnes Scott, Emory University, and Atlanta University. The Midwest: Ohio University, Chicago University, Indiana University, Iowa State, Kansas State. The Northeast: MIT, Yale, Harvard, Brown, Columbia, NYU, Rutgers, Boston University. The West: Texas Tech, Colorado State, Stanford University, SMU, UCLA,

THE POSSUM HUNTER

and Cal Tech. The Northwest: Washington State, the University of Oregon, Washington University.

As she pondered her offers, she considered their situation. Both she and her spouse, Mordecai, were simple people used to living simple country lives. Would they trade this for large urban environments filled with things of foreign nature to them? The only crime they had been touched by was Alonzo stealing a chicken and then getting caught or buying whiskey, beer, and wine from bootleggers. Adultery, rape, murder, and robbery were only things they read about in big cities.

In Hungerville there was no need for rape. Sex was free and available. Poor people don't rob poor people. What's the need? They would be foolish to try and rob the wealthy. Afterwards, where would they go? Where would they run to? Nobody got mad enough to kill anybody. For what? Nobody had anything to make someone envious of or jealous of. They were all poorer than owl shit.

For the sake of simplicity, she and Mordecai decided to remain in the state of Mississippi and let her pursue her Master's degree in mathematics at Mississippi State University in Starkville, Mississippi. Mordecai would use his G.I. Bill and enroll, too, in the department of husbandry—the care, cultivation, and breeding of crops and animals—farming. Although encouraged to do so by his favorite professor, Dr. Ernest Miles, he refused to try studying law or sociology.

This was a wise choice by Mordecai, for he was indeed suited for this field. The studies and fieldwork came as natural to him as strolling through the meadows, woods, corn and cotton fields of Hungerville. It fitted him like a glove on his hand. He had now mastered the artificial limb and walked as though it was normal. He was content with this even though there still existed inside of him the deep yearning to run through the meadows, fields, and woods in pursuit of possums and coons. He could not shake this desire in his pursuit of happiness.

Major roads through Starkville are U.S. Highway 82 and Mississippi Highways 12 and 25. Starkville is located in the northern part of the state close to the Tennessee state line in Oktibbeha County, Mississippi. Oktibbeha is a Native American word meaning either "bloody water" (because of a battle fought on the banks) or possibly "icy creek." It is surrounded by Choctaw, Webster, Clay, Noxubee, Lowndes, and Winston Counties. Mississippi State University is located there. It has the largest student enrollment in the state but, by far, is not the oldest college or university in the state. Mississippi College near Jackson holds that distinction.

Mordecai, who had now completely mastered his artificial limb, drove the Chevy along with Fannie Mae, to Starkville. Most of their belongings were packed into a U-Haul attached. They had decided to leave Willie, the baby (now three years old), with Fannie's parents until they got settled. He was a lovely child blessed with an exceedingly gifted mind and body coordination. He learned to walk, unassisted, at two; to talk, making complete sentences at two and a half; and to read at three. Would people who knew Mordecai's mentality question his inability to father such a genius? On several occasions Fannie thought about this? She could always say, "He took after his mother mentally and his father physically." He did, somehow, favor Mordecai a little bit. Willie could run, could jump, and had good body balance. He was destined to be a good coon and possum hunter, thought his uncle Alonzo, and he would see to that.

* * * * *

Dr. Fred Woullard had the following distinctions in 1970: (1) He had completed his undergraduate requirements with honors from Columbia University in New York; (2) He graduated summa cum laude from Johns Hopkins University's Medical School in Baltimore, Maryland. He shocked the world when he decided to do his internship at the University of Mississippi's Medical School in Jackson, Mississippi. This was considered a farce by his Johns Hopkins professors, an empty show, perhaps a comic show or play, involving ridiculously improbable situations and events!

They did not know of his love and concern for Fannie Mae who still resided in the state of Mississippi. They could not envision his feelings of guilt and betrayal to an innocent soul that he had impregnated and scandalized. With his own family honors achieved, he could now concentrate on righting the wrong he had caused. He did not know what had happened to Fannie after his departure and cowardice. He never knew of her reconciliation and marriage to Mordecai.

After enrolling in the University of Mississippi Medical School, he found a place to stay near Tougaloo. One day he decided to revisit the campus for old time's sake. While walking the campus of Tougaloo College, Fred's mind reminisced about walking and holding hands and kissing Fannie Mae beneath the cypress tree near Judson Cross Hall. His mind wandered about the sex they had in his Volkswagen that he still owned. Couldn't afford to get another car while he struggled to get through school in the Northeast. This was a gift from his grandparents in Alabama, encouraging him along.

He sat in the cafeteria and ate lunch with the students as in previous days. This was a good day, Friday, where they served fried fish and corn bread, sweet tea and cucumber salad, peas with onions, and banana pudding for dessert. Although the food in the Northeast was good, he had not forgotten the well-seasoned foods of the South. This food rekindled his taste buds and made him want to testify "Amen!"

Fred didn't think that he would see any of the students of his time frame that he knew but was shocked to see Bubba Johnson of Quitman, Mississippi still there. Bubba had not graduated and was still trying to fill the requirements for graduation.

"Hey, Fred, what's up? What you doing being back here on Tougaloo's campus?" asked Bubba as they shook hands.

"Well," answered Fred. "I was kinda looking for information on my old sweetheart, Fannie Mae Brown."

"Well, buy me a Coke and some peanuts and I'll 'school you' as much as I know," Bubba said.

They went into the canteen and sat down. Fred ordered a Coca Cola and a bag of Planters salted peanuts for Bubba. "Ain't you gonna have nothing, Fred?" asked Bubba.

"No," said Fred. "I just got through eating in the cafeteria."

"I hardly ever eat there. The food's just as bad as it was when you were here before, maybe even worse," exclaimed Bubba.

"No, it was good today, very good. Remember, today is Friday, and they still serve fried fish on Fridays."

"Um, hum."

"Now, tell me just what you know about Fannie Mae Brown."

"You mean Fannie Mae Johnson. She and Mordecai got married, right here on campus the Sunday after the day you left. Nobody could ever figger that out or understand why. Do you know why, Fred?"

"I think maybe I knocked her up and she had to marry somebody. Mordecai so happened to be the lucky or unlucky one depending on how you look at it. Lucky to have someone as beautiful and brilliant as Fannie is, or was, but unlucky to have to be a father to my child. I want her and the child. I mean to get them both."

"Mordecai would kill you, man, and she still is as pretty as she was the day or night you left. Both of them came back here and graduated last year. Mordecai is a Vietnam hero that lost his left leg in the war. He loves the baby boy and all three of them are closer than 'paint on a woodshed,'" Bubba said.

"I'll hate to break up such a cool family, but it must be done. When I finish my internship as a doctor, I can give her and my son a better life than they ever could dream of or imagine," said Fred.

"Well, what about Mordecai?" asked Bubba.

"As far as I'm concerned, Mordecai will be a lonesome possum hunter."

"On one leg?" asked Bubba.

"If it comes to that, so be it. I don't mean to sound unsympathetic, but it is my baby, and I love its mother. That's why I'm back in Mississippi, to make wrong right. If someone has to suffer, it won't be me, my baby, or Fannie Mae. Mordecai will have to pay the price." He continued, "That's the way the cookie crumbles."

* * * * *

It was April 1970 and all Mordecai had to do to complete his requirements for graduation was to pass two examinations, one in statistics and the other in advanced genetics. He knew that he didn't have a prayer of passing them on his own so he solicited Fannie Mae's help as usual. Being a disabled veteran, he was allowed to leave the classroom at his will to go escorted to the restroom. The person who escorted always waited outside the door while Mordecai "took care of business." Mordecai would smuggle the exam questions to the men's room where Fannie Mae waited, disguised as a male, in a commode area. He would leave her his papers, urinate and leave. Fannie Mae would solve the problems and answer the questions for him. About an hour later he would require another escort to the restroom where he would retrieve the answers. Needless to say, he passed the exams with flying colors and no one knew the less. Mordecai was indeed smart in his own way.

Fannie Mae, again, finished at the top of her class. This time she would choose Brown University to pursue her doctorate degree. Her plan was to get her doctorate out of the state of Mississippi at a very prominent school and then return to the prestigious state to teach at the University of Southern Mississippi or William Carey College, both located in Hattiesburg, a few miles from Hungerville where they planned to build an envious house of both beauty and comfort.

One month before commencement at Mississippi State, Fred Woullard had located the whereabouts of Fannie Mae and Mordecai. He had gone to the place that Fannie had led them—to the house of her parents in rural Forrest County. There he saw his baby and held him in his arms—and cried. When asked to explain his tears, he told what he considered the true story between he and Fannie Mae. A big "hush" fell upon the house as they began to wonder the outcome. He told them of his plan to marry their daughter, take excellent care of her and his son plus provide handsomely for them also, giving them a completely new house. Everybody seemed happy except Alonzo who declared that it was not Fred's baby but Mordecai's. He saw it in their feet—too much alike. Alonzo was good at examining feet of both coons and possums.

They told Fred that Mordecai and Fannie Mae were in Starkville attending Mississippi State University. Fred went to Starkville to Mississippi State's campus. There he disguised himself, followed their schedules and living habits. Mordecai was easily seen and located from a distance because of his prosthetics. They lived in a trailer about two miles northeast of the campus. They rode together when they both had classes the same day and returned together after classes. On the days that one had classes and the other didn't, the one who had classes would drive while the other stayed home unless someone needed to go to the library or to do research.

Tuesday morning as Mordecai drove to class, Fred observed him by binoculars. Fannie Mae was home alone. Fred waited until 10:00 a.m., then drove his Volkswagen to their trailer. He blew his horn, then got out. Fannie knew the sound of his horn from having heard it the many times he would come to pick her up at her dormitory. She knew the Volkswagen also but could not believe her eyes or ears. When she opened her door, there stood Fred Woullard as bright and as handsome as ever, not wearing anything on his head, thereby revealing his curly hair. She yelled "Fred!" and almost fainted as he grabbed her and lifted her to her feet. They kissed and then the world melted away. She moved back and said, "Fred, I'm a married woman now."

"I know," said Fred. "I know the whole story about y'all as told to me by two sources, Bubba Johnson and your folks. Fannie Mae, I'm almost a medical doctor now. I have finished my medical degree at Johns Hopkins and am now doing my internship here in Mississippi in Jackson. I chose Ole Miss Medical to be with you, to marry you and recognize our son. I have carried this guilt of neglect for years now. I apologize for running out on you when you needed me most, but I intend to make amends. I want you to divorce Mordecai and marry me so I can provide and take care of you and our child." He fell to his knees and begged and cried. "Please forgive me! Please marry me! I'm sorry!"

"Fred," she said. "It's not at all that simple. There is something I have to tell you that might make you hate me."

"No. Never could I hate you. I have planned and prayed to God for you to be mine and to be a good father to our child. What can make you say such a thing?"

"Fred, dear, it's not as simple as you think. Things are not as 'cut and dry' as they seem. Please sit down and let me explain." Fred sat.

"Perhaps it's me that needs to beg for forgiveness, for I have not been completely honest and truthful to you. You see, when I returned that summer from Brown University, I had just recently had sex with

THE POSSUM HUNTER

Fred spoke. "Not meaning to spoil an almost perfect afternoon/evening, I am compelled to tell you my reason for coming to see you. You would indeed make a fine father."

"Again, I don't quite understand you. Please don't speak in parables like our Savior Jesus. Come right out and say what you have to say," said Calvin.

Fred said, "Sure." After a brief pause, "Do you remember the fall semester of 1965 when you taught and tutored a beautiful brilliant exchange student from Tougaloo College in Mississippi? Her name was Miss Fannie Mae Brown."

"Yes, yes I recall quite vividly. She has one of the greatest minds that I ever encountered. We have recently offered her a stipend to pursue her doctorate degree here at Brown. We have reasons to believe that she shall accept our offer. Why do you ask?"

"When we were at Tougaloo then, she was my "main squeeze." On the day before she caught the train to return home, the two of you had unprotected sex. Two days later she arrived home. I picked her up and we, too, had unprotected sex. She became impregnated by one of us. I, cowardly thinking it was my fault, deserted her and returned to New York. Out of desperation, she married a student from her hometown to save her reputation and to give the baby a name. I have carried this burden of guilt ever since and planned to make amends. That is why I chose the University of Mississippi Medical Center to do my internship and continue in internal medicine. When I talked to her a few days ago, she told me about you two and the sexual encounter. She is not sure if the child is mine or yours. If it is not mine, but yours, I thought you should know."

Calvin Lucas looked as though he were in a hypnotic trance. He trembled as he dropped the drink he was holding as it slipped from his hand onto the table where it tumbled down to the floor. There it shattered. Kathleen noticed and came immediately to clean up the mess.

"I'm sorry, Kathleen," said Calvin. "Maybe I've had one drink too many."

"That's OK, Dr. Lucas. You don't have to explain. I'll take care of this. Want another drink?"

"Yes, yes," he replied. "This time make it a double Jack Daniels with no Coke."

Fred smiled and said, "Make that two, and I'm paying."

On the way back, Fred drove. Calvin asked, "When are you leaving, Dr. Woullard?"

"Tomorrow afternoon," replied Fred. "We can get your blood samples early tomorrow morning."

"Do you have a place to stay tonight?"

"No, but I will get one. I just thought I'd take care of first things first."

"Take a right at the next traffic light and drive five blocks to house number 1555 Roger Williams Street." He did.

They parked and rang the door bell, where a good-looking, charming elderly black lady admitted them. Her name was Mrs. Cleopatra Booker, a very good friend of Calvin, who owned the house.

"Cleo, this is a friend of mine, Dr. Fred Woullard, who needs a place to stay for one night only. He is in town on business that concerns me and will be flying out tomorrow evening for Atlanta. Can you put him up for tonight?

Cleo replied, "He can stay and I won't charge him anything. The whole second floor is vacant with three bedrooms to choose from. That young professor Adikin and his family moved out after he got his degree a week ago. Come in. Welcome, and are you hungry? I've got some Yankee pot roast left."

The mere mention of food made Fred and Calvin want to regurgitate. "No thanks, just finished eating," Calvin replied.

"Me, too," said Fred. "I feel the same as Dr. Lucas. Oh, ur, can't we call each other by our first names instead of the protocols of doctors?"

They shook hands. "Yes, Freddy. I'm Cal."

All three laughed as Cleopatra said, "And I'm Cleo."

As he started to depart, Calvin said, "Your car should be alright where it is parked on campus. I'll instruct security to keep a notice on it anyway. I'll pick you up tomorrow morning about what time?"

"About 5:30 or 6:00 a.m. You see, I'm an early riser. 'Early to bed, early to rise, makes a man healthy, wealthy, and wise.' Remember?"

THE POSSUM HUNTER

"Are you two certain that you don't care for something to eat now? I shall have breakfast waiting when you arrive tomorrow," said Cleo.

"No, no, nothing more tonight, please," Fred replied.

"Cain't eat anymore, eh?" Calvin asked. Then he continued as he began to take his departure (emulating Southern colored folks), "At first you wuz as hunger as a Go—rilla. Now you is as full as a Irish tick." They all laughed. He left.

Fred returned to Jackson, Mississippi, the next night with refrigerated samples of Dr. Calvin Lucas's blood.

Calvin had almost recovered from his shock and was dying to hear the test results. He always dreamed of becoming a father even though he was still not married. His steady date now was Dr. Loren Hunter of his department, the same one who helped escort Fannie Mae with him to Newport that night. She was beautiful but Caucasian. He could not bring himself to propose to her. If they were to marry, he'd have to take her to Birmingham, Alabama on occasions. How would the people there react? Would the whites and blacks be hostile? Would they welcome them with open arms? They were often stared at even here in Rhode Island. He would wait.

* * * * *

In two weeks Fannie Mae met with Fred at the university's Medical Center in Jackson.

Mordecai had field study to do so he could not go on this urgent trip to Hungerville. Fannie tried to explain the urgency of the situation to Mordecai but he could not agree. First, he resented that Fred had visited his house while he wasn't home. He thought of Louis Jordan's song, "I'm gonna move way on the outskirts of town, cause I don't want nobody always hanging around. I don't need no ice man, gonna buy me a fridgedare."

Mordecai—"What does it matter who the real daddy is? I love 'Little Willie' and have accepted him as my own. I believe that he loves me. If I diddn' know better, I would swear that he is mine."

Fannie Mae—"You see, honey, it's important for me to know and perhaps Little Willie later on in life. If he or the real father ever became sick and needed blood or something like a kidney or lung transplant, both would be available instantly. Besides, I would like to know for myself." She cried and Mordecai consented.

"Well, go head," he said. "But I want to tell you that no man could ever love you and the baby no more than I do." He continued, "I have field work to do and can't go with you. Give your folks and Little Willie my love. I'll have someone to pick me up."

"No, no," Fannie replied. "I'll drive a Hertz rent-a-car. We can afford it. I'll put it on our MasterCard or our Visa." They had climbed up another notch. Nobody they associated with or knew in Hungerville had a credit card. If they did, they could use them at the boss man's store and keep better records. Or would they run wild and charge themselves into even more debt?

Fannie Mae drove home, picked Little Willie up, and brought him back to Jackson's Medical Center where they met Dr. Fred Woullard. They all shook hands and went immediately to the laboratory where samples of blood were drawn. The samples were placed alongside the samples of Dr. Calvin Lucas's of Brown University.

It was 11:30 a.m. and almost lunch time when Fred came up with this not so brilliant idea of them returning to Tougaloo to dine. It could have been a beautiful rendezvous or nostalgic event except that they had no idea that today's event at Tougaloo was graduation day.

When they arrived on campus, there was hardly any room to park. Luckily they knew the campus and maneuvered between cars and trees to a spot that they had used while students to make love. They parked and walked to the auditorium.

On their way to, at the auditorium, and afterwards, they ran into several of their former acquaintances to whom they tried to explain their being together. "Coincidence" was the lie they told. Both came to commencement and just happened to run into each other. They didn't try to hide. What's the use? They all three attended the reception afterwards where they loaded their bellies with food and drinks. The biggest surprise was the graduation of Bubba Johnson of Quitman. He had finally met all of the college's requirements and became an alumnus. They both congratulated him. Fred shook his hand and Fannie Mae hugged him.

"What ya'll do with Mordecai?" he asked.

"He's alright," said Fannie. "He's at home and couldn't come but I'll give him your regards when I return to Starkville tonight."

"Ya'll still together?"

"Certainly. Fred and I just happened to bump into each other."

He whispered to her, "Well, that ain't the way Fred explained it to me. He said he was gonna get you to quit Mordecai and marry you and take care of his child."

"That has not happened and if it does happen, you'll be one of the first to know."

They departed in different directions. She would wait a while at the car giving Fred ample time to walk to the road off campus.

When she picked Fred up she said, "Fred, we have to hurry. It's almost 4:00 and I have to drive back to Hattiesburg, then to Starkville."

Fred replied, "Let me simplify the situation. You go on back to Starkville from here and I'll drive Little Willie to Hattiesburg. After all, he is probably my son anyway."

Little Willie seemed perplexed by the whole day's affairs. His ingenious mind would have to have answers. In due time he would get them.

* * * * *

September 1, 1970, Mordecai and his family arrived in Providence, Rhode Island to find a place to stay while his wife matriculated for her doctorate degree at Brown University. The baby was now almost three years old. They sought a place not too far from the university where they would not have to negotiate snow driving for too long a distance. They stayed in a hotel downtown while they struggled to secure an apartment. There were several perfect prospects listed almost within walking distance from the university that were suddenly filled just before their arrival. They were unaware of New England prejudices and never considered their color to be their hindrance. They thought that all Yankees loved Negroes.

Out of desperation they sought out Dr. Calvin Lucas. He invited them into his office which now had a painting of Euclid of Alexandria portrayed as a black African. "Come in, please, and please be seated." He embraced them all. "Fannie Mae, you have not changed over these years. You still are as pretty and as vibrant as you were four years ago. And your mind has even grown sharper. Summa cum laude at both Tougaloo and Mississippi State plus a perfect score on our doctorate's candidate's exam. This makes you the smartest student that I've ever taught. Even the Caucasians and Asian candidate did not "max" the exam. How may I be of service to you now? School doesn't start until two weeks from now."

"Calvin, uh, urn, I mean Dr. Lucas, this is my son, Little Willie Johnson, and my spouse, Mordecai Johnson. They have accompanied me to pursue my doctorate, but for the love of God, we cannot find a suitable place of living within a twenty-mile radius of this campus. Places are listed as being vacant but when we get there, they are filled. We are desperate."

"It's because of the color of your skin. Some of these people cover their prejudices with soft voices and smiles. They are no different from rednecks in Birmingham, Alabama or Starkville, Mississippi. We could sue them, but you don't have enough time and certainly you don't want to be confronted with these issues while studying. I assure you that our programs are among the most challenging in the world. No school is better than us. Many are inferior to us."

All this time Mordecai had not spoken. He then spoke. "Maybe we should go back down South where white people don't hide their prejudices. They come right out and say, 'Nigger, I don't like you.' Then you know where you stand."

Calvin ordered them cookies, milk, coffee, cream with real sugar, then picked up the phone. He spoke into the phone. "Mrs. Booker, this is Dr. Calvin Lucas. How are you?"

"I'm fine, Calvin, and you can drop that Dr. shit." They both laughed hysterically.

THE POSSUM HUNTER

"Is your second floor still available? I got a good-looking black family who will need a place to stay for perhaps three years or more. A husband, wife, and a three-year-old baby. They are all from Mississippi, and I recommend them highly. The wife is smarter than a whip and will be entering our doctorate program in math in two weeks.

"Now, Calvin, you have touched my weak spots. You know how I love children and how much I care for the poor Southern colored folks. That's why I got myself banged and bruised riding those Freedom Buses from Virginia to Texas until I couldn't take it anymore and came on back home where the people hide their true feelings about you."

He replied, "That's exactly what I'm talking about. They have spent a good part of two weeks looking for a place to stay but when they get there, the doors are closed—no room at the inn." That's when he looked at them and opened his arms, using the gesture "Am I correct?" He asked, "Do you have the money to pay?" They assured him that money was no object.

Mrs. Booker said, "Ask them can they afford four hundred dollars a month plus utilities?" They said they could and would she accept three months' rent in advance?

Mrs. Booker shouted but only Calvin heard her. "I shall bring them over shortly so you can meet them," he said.

Calvin continued, "You now have a place to stay two blocks away from here. If, for any reason, it doesn't suit you, you have another option of living here on campus in our married couples units with one, two, or three bedrooms. They run about five hundred dollars a month. Your stipend will pay you two hundred fifty a month plus food for one person."

They breathed a sigh of relief. "Before we go, tell us a little something about Mrs. Booker."

"Cleopatra Booker is a very sweet, semi-wealthy, black lady about sixty-two years old. She is a widow who lost her husband ten years ago in a boating accident. He was both a lobster and shrimp fisherman who made very good money and provided for her and their three children handsomely. He purchased the house she now lives in during the fifties and it's paid for. She sent all of her children to all-black colleges in the north—Howard University in Washington, D.C., Morgan State in Baltimore, Maryland, and Central State in Ohio. She was afraid of the South but tried to make amends by becoming a Freedom Rider. She has paid her dues. All her kids graduated from college but never returned home to stay. She is lonely and loves people, especially children. The fisherman's union had all of their workers insured, so she received about $300,000 for the death of her husband, Josh Booker, her high school sweetheart. When I first came to Brown to teach, there is where I stayed. She is like a surrogate mother to me. I met her at church while living in a dormitory. She rescued me and took me in. We are friends for life. I have even taken her home with me to Birmingham at Thanksgiving and Christmas. She marvels over the southern cooking but is an expert herself on New England dishes. Her clam chowder and lobster bisque are truly exquisite and luxurious. I hope you are hungry for she is trained in pot luck dinners. Her house is always prepared for the unexpected visitors."

Certified Letter from Dr. Fred Woullard to Dr. Calvin Lucas

Fred M. Woullard
997 Hanging Moss Street
Tougaloo, MS
August 20, 1970

Dr. Calvin Lucas, Ph.D.
Department of Applied Mathematics
Brown University
182 George Street
Providence, Rhode Island

THE POSSUM HUNTER

Dear Cal,

I, Sherlock Holmes, have not yet solved the mystery. The blood tests proved nothing except that we both can be the father. Your blood type is "AB" and mine is "AB" also. The baby's blood type is "A," so we are right back where we started. Either one of us can be the father. We will just have to hold on until something new is discovered.

You can tell Fannie yourself. She has decided to pursue her doctorate degree at Brown University, there with you.

Sincerely,

Freddy

At 1555 Angella Street, Calvin Lucas parked his four door Buick sedan and escorted his passengers to the door, then rang the doorbell where the chimes played "Dixie." This was a reminder of her years as a Freedom Rider and always provoked a conversation which Cleopatra desired. Way down inside of her were deep inner feelings of guilt for not having been born in the South nor ever having any roots there at all. All of her and her husband's kin came from Africa to Rhode Island. As slaves escaped from the docked ship on its way to Jamaica, they were lucky enough to be captured by the descendants of the founder of the state, Roger Williams. The founder of Rhode Island, Roger Williams, fled the oppressive Puritanism of the Massachusetts Bay colony and established a tradition of religious toleration, along with prickly resistance to all forms of tyranny in his new colony.

Their captors were Baptist, who, in 1638, became the first Baptist church in America, established in Providence by dissenters from the Puritan church in Massachusetts. To the Baptists, slavery was abominable, so they hid and cared for them until the ship sailed away to Jamaica. On their journeys back to Africa, the ships would often stop in Rhode Island to unload molasses made in Jamaica by slaves, to

S. EARL WILSON, III

produce rum which was shipped to Africa for the purchasing of more slaves. The Triangle of Despair: Africa—The West Indies—Rhode Island. Newport had twenty-one rum distilleries.

Cleopatra Booker knew that her state, even though it had fought valiantly for America during the Revolutionary War, the Tripoli War in 1801, the War of 1812 with England, the Mexican War of 1846, and the Civil War, was equally guilty of enhancing slavery and the degradation of African's souls. This was the belief she held, that provoked her to make amends for, by becoming a Freedom Rider.

The door opened. There stood Mrs. Cleopatra Booker in all her splendor, wearing expensive apparels, golden earrings, and an African ornament worn around her neck. Her hair was natural in an "Afro" style with hints of grey. Her smile was radiant and her face was pretty. Before anyone could speak, she said, "Hello, y'all, I'm Cleo Booker and yes and no, I'm from Dixie, even though I was not born there. My heart is there where the black author, Richard Wright, wrote, 'Is it true what they say about Dixie? Does the sun really shine all the time? Do the sweet magnolias blossom at everybody's door? Do the folks keep eating possum 'til they can't eat no more?'" Then she laughed as everybody else smiled. She embraced all three, then took the baby in her arms and cuddled him. "Little Willie" went to her willingly. The love bond between him and her was immediately established.

"Mrs. Booker," Mordecai spoke, "I'm Mordecai Johnson. This is my wife Fannie Mae and our son Willie M. Johnson." They all embraced again.

"Before we eat, let me show you the house and the second floor where you will possibly be living."

Mordecai spoke again and said, "I surely appreciate that poem you just quoted about people eating possums. It broke down all barriers and we feel quite at home even here in New England. Do y'all eat possums here too?"

"Un ucha," Calvin said.

The second floor seemed like an enclosed veranda with plenty of walking and living space. It had a full-size kitchen and dining room, three medium size bedrooms close to each other, two with only a door separating them. This would be ideal for them and the baby. Two and a half bathrooms and a spacious living/entertainment room. It had a back door entrance where they could come and leave without interfering with the front entrance. It was just ideal, with the use of a three car garage. Mrs. Booker would require only one space for her Cadillac Coupe Deville.

They sat at her table in the kitchen for some of her pot luck food prepared in advance for the unexpected visitors—perhaps the expected visitors.

"When the unexpected becomes the expected, it makes the unexpected the expected." These words of wisdom shocked everybody coming from the mouth of Mordecai, who was thought to be unwise. What he said was surely not expected.

Cleo, as she told everybody to call her, had meticulously prepared clam chowder so succulent that the word delicious is replaced by scrumptious. She made it with real cheese, smoked bacon, thyme and bay leaves. This was followed by roasted crab cakes with creamy lobster sauce. The main entrée was roasted shrimp pomodoro, consisting of roasted shrimp seasoned with lemon and white pepper, served over whole wheat spaghetti with a traditional pomodoro sauce made with fire-roasted tomatoes, white wine and chopped garlic alongside an Italian blend of carrots, cauliflower and zucchini. Everyone's minds were blown away, including Calvin's, who was no stranger to her cooking.

They decided that this was the place they wanted to live and did so for the three years that it took for Fannie to receive her doctorate degree. This meal was only the tip of the iceberg; many more flavorsome New England meals would follow.

* * * * *

Cleo was a built-in babysitter who would accept no pay, so the two of them were free to do what was demanded of them and to go and come as they pleased.

What was Mordecai to do as his wife pursued her degree? His artificial leg would disqualify him from good paying jobs that required physical labor. He dared not to try and matriculate for any degree at Brown. After being turned down for so many jobs, he again became desperate. He would not go again to Dr. Lucas after having been told by Fannie Mae of their interlude. She decided he should know also. Mordecai became upset and declared her a "whore." She retaliated by saying, "Yes, I was promiscuous but not unfaithful to you but to Fred Woullard while you were busy screwing Bessie Mae Graham and Gizelle Haniford. And remember it was you who put me down and not the other way around." She continued to hide her guilt of already seeing Fred Woullard behind his back. "It was you who broke my heart at the canteen that day."

Mordecai agreed and became sullen and gloomily silent. What she said was true, he agreed, and after all, she was then no longer his girl but Fred's and didn't even have to tell him about Calvin but she did. At least she is honest and "up front" with me and hasn't messed with anyone else since we reunited. "But I'm sick and tired of this who the daddy really is shit. If and when we do find out, perhaps we should give Little Willie to him or we can get a divorce and let you marry the real father," exclaimed Mordecai.

Fannie Mae broke down into tears and said, "Oh, Mordecai, my darling husband, I love you so much I could never think of life without you. I would never leave you for another but it would break my heart to part with my child."

"Well, then, why don't you stop thinking of him as your child but as our child. I love him no matter who the daddy is. Let's have another child now just in case." They embraced, kissed, prayed together, and made unprotected love. Fannie Mae knew that getting pregnant and giving birth was not a wise decision at this time while pursuing her demanding requirements for her Ph.D. but she did it for the love of Mordecai.

It was then the middle of September. If they conceived now, the baby should be born in June. They would have from June until the following September to care for the baby unassisted (partially—there was always Cleo). They would ask her sister, Mae Helen, or her mother,

THE POSSUM HUNTER

Sally T., to come live with them for a year to help take care of the baby and would pay them a salary if they accepted.

It was her mother, Sally T., who came and she would not accept any salary, only occasionally some "chunk change," that is, ten to fifteen dollars "every now and then." Sometimes they permitted her to "shop till she dropped," running into the hundreds of dollars but they didn't mind. It was still a cheap bargain.

After completing her coursework that year with all A's, Fannie Mae gave birth on July 4, 1971, to a 5 pound 4 ounce beautiful, bubbly baby girl whom Mrs. Booker, by her own request, named Rosa Michelle Johnson. She wanted to break from the country traditional Southern naming list. She didn't know that she would be called upon to repeat this gesture two more times.

After spending a year and a half in Providence, Sally T. went on back home. She had accomplished her mission of being with, and caring for, her child and her grandbaby. She also relished the reunion with Little Willie. She got them started, showed them what to do and how to do. At times she challenged Mrs. Booker in cooking (sometimes winning).

It was Christmas vacation time when Mordecai and Fannie Mae loaded her and all her things into their station wagon and drove them home. Sally T. had purchased clothing and items from Providence's malls and stores to use and give away. There would be cosmetics, dresses, skirts, blouses, underwear, blue jeans, shoes, and stockings for she and Mae Helen and Ethyl Mae. There would be caps, hats, shirts, sport coats, ties, britches, overalls, belts, suspenders, socks, shoes, underwear, and a suit apiece for Lonzo, Jim, and Johnnie B. plus her husband, Amos C. The items consisted of fingernail clippers, can openers, bottle openers, a tool box, a barber set for them to cut their own hair, a modern radio, and a television set, an iron, and ironing board. There was plenty of New England canned food like clam chowder, lobster bisque, oysters, and stew. She also took home some New England wine and cheese.

They would bring back Mordecai's mother Rebecca who didn't want to be outdone by Sally T. She wanted bragging rights too. This could go a long ways at "big meeting time" at church revivals.

S. EARL WILSON, III

* * * * *

It was the month of October and Mordecai was on his knees praying in the living room downstairs when Mrs. Booker and Sally T. walked in with Little Willie. As he ended his prayer, he said, "Lord, please help me now. This I ask in the name of Your son, Jesus. Amen!" He arose and was startled to see them standing there. "Excuse me," he said. "I didn't mean to change your living room to a prayer room. I should have gone upstairs to my room."

"No need for an apology. Any room in this dwelling is suited for God."

"Amen," said Sally T. "Yes, Jesus." She was ready to hold church.

"I know that prayers are private things. I heard you ask for help. Is there anything that I may be able to do to help you?" asked Cleo.

"Mrs. Booker, I'm as desperate as I was when seeking a place to stay in Providence. I need to work but cannot for the love of God find a job. Maybe its because I'm colored or maybe it's because I'm handicapped but I can't find work. I have enough money saved and from my disability to pay you and survive but a man has pride. I want not only to support my family but to also give them amenities and extras. Besides, a child should not be brought up seeing his daddy hanging around the house not working. He needs someone who sets examples to go by. Understand?"

"Yes, I understand. Perhaps God sent me to help you. I know a lot of people, and I have a lot of resources in Providence. Now let's see—you have a degree from Tougaloo and your Master's from Mississippi State, don't you?" she asked.

"Yes, ma'am," he answered. "My undergraduate degree is in political science with a minor in physical education. My Master's degree is in animal husbandry."

"Well, then, I think you qualify to teach school. You could teach high school or junior high school social studies or political science. Your animal husbandry qualifies you to teach biology. I have friends on the school board and I know two black principals. I'll invite all of them over Friday night for a little something to eat and drink, then I'll introduce you and your family to them and recommend you to teach. Is that okay with you?"

"Yes, it is," said Mordecai. That day was Wednesday, plenty of time till Friday.

*****

By luck or by the grace of God, they all accepted Mrs. Booker's invitation. So did Dr. Calvin Lucas, Department Head of Mathematics at Brown University, whom she had mentioned would be present.

She served cocktails that Mordecai mixed superbly—oysters American style prepared and served by Fannie Mae, Sally T., and Cleo—broiled oysters and bacon: en brochette: oysters wrapped in bacon, alternated on skewers with mushrooms dipped in egg and breadcrumbs, broiled and served with mai d' hotel butter; mussels French style: a la Francaise: precooked mussels, marinated in oil, vinegar, pepper and mustard powder, served very cold.

Then they all sat down to a scrumptious meal of New England lobster in lobster sauce—whole lobster tail (out of the shell) topped with a creamy lobster sauce made with white wine, tarragon and thyme, served with oven-roasted vegetables and a seasoned blend of white and wild rice. All of these things were new to Sally but she retained them.

Their conversations centered around the education of American youth as expected, their weakness in science and math as compared to other countries. From there to the introduction of the disabled decorated war hero, Mordecai, his credentials, background, and pretty wife who was a topnotch student at Brown pursuing her doctorate degree in math to their accelerated kids and Mordecai's inability to find work and his wishes to become a school teacher.

The first person to react was the black middle school principal., Ed. Education Providence University, Dr. John E. Harrison. He could use a black man of his diversity and caliber as a social studies teacher and assistant track coach. He could, perhaps, also use him in the sciences.

"First come, first served." Mordecai accepted Dr. Harrison's offer. Dr. Harrison, along with the school's superintendent, instructed him on how to apply for Rhode Island's teaching certification. He would be hired the ensuing Monday as a probationary teacher and would be given professional status when he finished the required courses. He would be given two years to complete the courses desired—thirty hours. There were night courses, weekend courses, and workshops offered. Many first year teachers received their Master's degrees after completing the requirements. They just had to enroll in a college such as Providence College or Rhode Island College, Johnson and Wales University, or Brown. Most did not choose Brown University. Her qualifications and courses were too stringent.

* * * * *

Moving from middle school to high school, Mordecai became a successful track coach and a dynamite social studies teacher who not only taught about Southern politics, civil rights, the Vietnam War, his lost limb, but also the enhancement of slavery by Rhode Island. After returning from trips to Mississippi for the Christmas holidays, he would often bring back to his students stalks of sugarcane to chew and sassafras roots to boil for tea. The students became ecstatic. He also would bring back caps and tee shirts of Mississippi and other Southern schools to give away as rewards for academic accomplishment. These caps of Mississippi State, Ole Miss, University of Southern Mississippi (USM), Jackson State, Tougaloo, Millsap, Alcorn, Alabama, LSU, and Tennessee were the highlights. When worn by the students, they stood apart from the colleges and universities in the Northeast and caused much discussion. It made them unique. It was an attention magnet. The unnoticed became noticed. The little student became big, and the ugly could attract the pretty by offering to give or to share the wearing of the apparel.

Mr. Johnson was a dynamite teacher and the news spread. He was "Teacher of the Week, Month, and Year" more than once. His greatest honor was in 1976 when the yearbook was dedicated to him. In all his humbleness and humility, he cried. Fannie Mae and Mrs. Booker attended this dedication ceremony along with Dr. John E. Harrison, the principal who first hired him. They were all proud of his accomplishments.

After being handed his personal copy and introduced by the president of the student body, Mordecai spoke to an audience composed of the mayor, principals, superintendents, students, news reporters, television personnel with their cameras, board of education members, PTA members, religious personnel—Catholic, Presbyterian, Jews, Baptists, Methodists, and other faiths.

He spoke well, the speech that Fannie Mae had helped him write, that he had rehearsed a hundred times:

"Good morning, ladies and gentlemen."

"Good morning," they replied.

"On occasions such as this, it is proper protocol to give recognition first to the highest echelon, then work downward to the lowest echelon. For instance, first recognizing the mayor of our great city of Providence, the school's superintendents, principals, faculty members, etc. But today I shall do something to the converse."

"My first recognition goes to the students of Roger Williams High. Will all of you please stand?" They all stood and whistled and yelled. The whole audience applauded and also stood.

"Thank you. Our gracious mayor, our competent superintendent, my principal Dr. Williams—I said my principal and not our principal, though she is both yours and mine, because Dr. Sue Williams has been a strong supporter of me since I joined her faculty two years ago. It was she, in fact, who recruited me to come to such an excellent environment of learning. Sue, I thank you. Notwithstanding, could I not give credence to our competent faculty members. Thank you for your support." Everybody applauded.

"I thank you from the innermost part of my heart for the greatest honor that I have received in my life, second only to the marriage to my wife, Mrs. Fannie Mae Johnson. Please stand." She stood, and the audience stood and clapped their hands.

"When I was a student at Tougaloo College in Mississippi, I earned a first place gold medal for winning the one hundred yard dash in the "Tuskegee Relays" in a record breaking time. That's when I had two legs." He smiled. Nobody else did. A few shed tears. "That medal," he continued, "was then the highlight of my life."

"This yearbook dedication overshadows my past events a thousand times. Had it not been for Dr. Calvin Lucas who introduced me to the elegant Mrs. Cleopatra Booker who introduced me to Dr. John E. Harrison, this never could have happened. Me thinks each of you is God sent, especially you, Cleo. Will each of you please stand?" They all stood and applause ricocheted from the walls to the ceiling.

"Mr. Peter Rosenberg, president of the student body, and all of the students of Roger Williams High, I am humble and grateful to be the recipient of this great award that others like Benjamin Rosenstock of the mathematics department, Josh Baker of the science department, Elizabeth Shoemaker of the English department, Coach Eddie Davidson of the physical education and athletic department who won us a state championship in soccer last year, Edmond Brown, Alice Whitter, Nancy Gatewood, and anyone on our staff could have and should have received."

"Gratitude is sometimes best shown in silence. Please join me in a moment of silence."

Nothing was said for two minutes or more. It was so quiet that you could hear a gnat breathe. Or a mouse urinate on cotton. Mordecai then broke the silence by stepping down and saying, "Muchas gracias, merci beau-coup, danke-schon, ar:gato, and thank you very much."

All of them, Mordecai, Fannie, Calvin, Little Willie, Cleo, and Dr. Harrison watched themselves on the televised evening news while they shared pot luck dinner prepared by Fannie Mae who emulated Cleo's style almost to perfection, plus her own of Southern fried chicken. Her meal:

First course:Iced melon, caviar, smoked salmon bits.
Second course:Consommé.
Third course:Mississippi fried chicken, New England mashed potatoes, green beans with onions and carrots, baked bread.
Dessert:A combination of fresh fruit and ice cream.
Drinks:White wine and/or sweet tea.

THE POSSUM HUNTER

Nobody complained, and Calvin thought about what it would be like if the child was his and if he were married to Fannie Mae. His conscious got the better part of him, yet the thought intrigued him. He recalled their first, and only, sexual encounter with a woman who could cook like this!

*****

1976 was three years after Ph.D. Fannie Mae Johnson had received her doctorate from Brown University and Mr. Roscoe Mordecai Johnson had completed all his requirements to become a Rhode Island certified teacher. Their baby child, Rosa, was seven years old. Little Willie was nine and attended the Rhode Island School for the Gifted. Mordecai was granted tenure at a salary of $20,000 a year plus a coaching bonus of $1,200. Fannie Mae accepted the position of Associate Professor of Mathematics at Providence College at a salary of $35,000 per year. Their total income, including Mordecai's disability check, was $70,600. Since they were not "fast life" people, they did not spend foolishly or live extravagantly. They saved and invested moderately in stocks and bonds. They now had superseded all of Hungerville's workers tenfold or more.

Mrs. Booker cried the year of 1978 when they moved from her dwelling into a house of their own. She had become attached to all of them and loved them like her own family. She would miss the "pitty patter" of little feet running to and fro, the adult companionship, conversations, and dining together. Mordecai and Fannie cried, too, but it was time to move on. The good Lord had provided Mrs. Booker as a steppingstone for their accomplishments, and they were both grateful indeed. They promised to keep in touch and co-visit often.

If Little Willie and Rosa were sad, they didn't show it. They just kept on playing together, sometimes yelling and screaming. Mrs. Booker didn't mind. She enjoyed playing along with them at times. She especially enjoyed playing games of mental skills at which Rosa and Willie both excelled. Rosa seemed to be as "bright" or "brighter" than Little Willie. This ain't supposed to be. Mordecai was her real daddy.

They planned to bring Mae Helen or Ethyl Mae, or both, to live with them in their five bedroom house to assist in living conditions, to baby sit their children, and to expose them (sisters) to cultural life outside of Hungerville. Perhaps with their beauty and Mississippi education (Jackson College and Alcorn) they could find a suitable husband on the high echelon. They certainly would have the exposure.

Sally T. had long since been gone back home, loaded down with her goodies too. "Rebecca didn't have nothing on her!" Both she and Rebecca had been given one thousand dollars cash to take with them—"Hallelujah! Praise the Lord!"

* * * * *

July 4, 1976, on Rosa's birthday, four years before the use of DNA, deoxyribonucleic acid, the truth maker, the only real fantastic test to prove true fatherhood, Mordecai, his family, Fannie Mae, Little Willie, Rosa, and Cleo Booker were all on a ferry boat leaving from Point Judith carrying their picnic basket filled with goodies and an ice chest filled with their favorite drinks headed to Block Island, Rhode Island. Neither of them had ever heard of, or cared about, DNA that, four years later, would reveal Little Willie's true father. What will happen when the truth is finally revealed? Stay tuned!

Block Island is a small island between the Block Island sound and the Atlantic Ocean. It is a fun-filled island full of recreation and relaxation places. For surfers, there is Surfers Beach, the best on the island for waves. For observers, there is Nathan Mott Park, Block Island's oldest park, teeming with wildlife. Great Salt Pond holds a very large marina—a small boat basin where supplies and moorings are available, having a service station and frequently other facilities such as sleeping accommodations, restaurants, stores, and amusements.

All, except Mordecai, would rent and ride bicycles. He would use a four wheeler with a trailer attached for his mode of transportation. To enjoy this island, one needs to move on his or her very own as willed. To hire or to wait on transportation is a "drag." Besides, Mordecai could transport the picnic basket and cooler along with himself. It was

THE POSSUM HUNTER

a fun-filled day that each of them enjoyed. They rode. They swam. They ate. They drank. They played. They observed. They relaxed. Before they retired for the night in their hotel, the tired, happy group let Rosa blow out the candles on her birthday cake, served some of it along with ice cream, sang "Happy Birthday," and gave her presents. Rosa, sleepy-eyed and happy, kissed everyone and said, "I love you, Mommy and Daddy. I love you, Mrs. Cleo, and I guess I love you, too, Little Willie. Thank you all very much." A tear fell from Little Willie's eye. He loved his little sister.

July 4, 1976, four years before DNA, Dr. Calvin Lucas, too, was at Block Island but he and Professor Loren Hunter spent the entire day at Surfers Beach waterskiing. They were both avid skiers, summer and winter. Both had read about DNA, but it didn't quite seem to concern their mathematical minds now. It would affect them vastly in four years. Good or bad?

They swam. They surfed. They ate cherrystone clams on half shell and crab cakes, and they drank wine and beer. They spent the night together, swam and rode bikes the next morning, ate brunch and caught the ferry back to Narraganset Bay, where their car was parked.

As they rode back to Providence, Calvin's mind wandered from Loren to Fannie Mae, trying to decide which one would be the better mate for him. Both of them had the intelligence he desired in a woman. Both were accelerated mathematicians like him. There would be no clash of careers and both were beautiful and attractive. Their offspring would have to possess good minds and above normal intelligence.

Calvin was a lover and a connoisseur of good foods. Loren could prepare exotic dishes that he loved, but man, could Fannie Mae fry up some chicken! He would be happy with either. He wished that he could have both. Maybe polygamy wasn't so bad after all.

July 4, 1976—Tougaloo College held a fund-raising picnic that day from 12:00 p.m.—5:00 p.m. Their spread was magnificent with potato salad, corn on the cob, green salad, green beans, baked beans, light bread, barbecue ribs and chicken, smoked sausage, tea, lemonade, soft drinks, and beer. Yes, they had now reached the stage where beer could be consumed openly. There was ice cream, cake, pie and watermelon for "sweets."

A musical trio from Jackson College played dance music while people ate and danced. The trio consisted of a pianist, a drummer, and a saxophone player, exceedingly good. Tougaloo didn't charge an admission fee and had announced it well, sent out invitations to most of its alumni, advertised it on television and radio. Those who attended were expected to make contributions at the end of this glorious event. The contributions came to nine thousand one hundred dollars for the scholarship/building funds.

Among this crowd attending was Gizzele Hanniford and Dr. Fred Woullard. Gizzele, still beautiful, was a successful entrepreneur who owned beauty salons in both Greenwood and Jackson, Mississippi, with expectations of opening another in Hattiesburg. Gizelle was never one to sit back and wait for the action to come to her. If it didn't happen within a certain amount of time, she would initiate it herself. When she saw this handsome doctor, Fred Woullard, dancing with Bertha Dishman, her classmate, she didn't hesitate to interfere. She moved across the floor while dancing with Bubba Johnson, bumping into Fred and Bertha, and said, "Y'all mind changing partners?" Nobody objected, so they switched partners. As if she willed it, the trio switched to a slow piece. She then melted into Fred's arms and clung to him as if by magnet. They have been together ever since.

Fred knew that since 1944 that DNA had been declared the blueprint of heredity and followed the study closely. He had already predicted that it, one day, would solve his problem when details could be worked out.

He and Gizzelle lived together. They "shacked up" but did not marry. He still hoped for Fannie Mae. If, if?

July 4, 1976, Hungerville, Mississippi, Section A, outside of Hattiesburg, Mississippi, in Forrest County. Hungerville, Sections B and C, are divided between Jones, Perry, Lamar, Pearl River, and Stone Counties.

The Allison's plantation's party, given annually on the Fourth of July, was simply referred to as "The Fourth." It was a humongous affair that people in that vicinity looked forward to, hosted by the rich Allison family: the father, Thomas; his wife, Peggy; and their three children, Rosemary, the oldest at 32, Fredrick Jr., 30, and the prettiest, Suzanne, now 28.

They all still lived there because actually there was nowhere else that was better. Their houses were large, spacious, and beautiful, with pools. Their bank accounts were bountiful, and they traded new cars of their choice every two years. Their hired help did all of the manual labor, both whites and blacks. They attended Broadway plays in New York, Mardi Gras in New Orleans, Mobile, and Rio, skied in New Hampshire and Colorado, swam in Biloxi, Los Angeles, Gulfport, Jamaica, and the French Riveria. They shopped in London, Rome, Paris, Minnesota, Houston, and New Jersey. Where else would their lives be any better? They drank beer in Ireland and in Scotland. They drank Scotch and played golf. Oh, well.

On the Fourth of July, they were very patriotic. Their lawns were decorated with colors of red, white and blue. They simply called their affair "THE FOURTH!" There was live music, and the bands alternated, some playing "Dixie," "God Bless America," and country music. Occasionally, an authentic Grand Ole Opry star would play and sing, someone like Conway Twitty. It must have cost them a "pretty penny," but what the hell, they could well afford it. There were rock bands and blues bands also.

High class friends and peasants all were invited. They all could mingle if desired. Some did, some didn't. Most of the black folks kept to themselves except when lining up to get food. The food consisted of two or three whole roasted pigs on a rotisserie, carved by a worker who sacrificed his free day for double pay as did all of the workers; barbecued ribs, barbecued link sausages, barbecued goats, barbecued chickens and fowls and steaks were served. There were cases and kegs of cold beer. There was wine and whiskey plus lemonade and soft drinks. There were potato salad and baked beans and gumbo and fried fish and watermelon galore.

There was horseback riding, horseshoe games, touch football and softball games, checkers and chess.

This was one way of saying "thanks" to friends, sharecroppers, and workers. They looked forward to hosting the "Fourth" each year, and people looked forward to attending each year. This stupendous event lasted until night, until the fireworks show was over. The next day was a free day and welcomed by those who drank too much alcohol. It was also a chance to make some extra money by being a part of the cleanup crew.

Although Block Island was great, Fannie and Mordecai wished that their children could experience the Fourth as they had done.

Not breaking family traditions, all three of the Allison's children attended Mississippi State University and graduated with honors. Rosemary, during her junior year at State, ran into somebody she thought she knew in the school's cafeteria. It was Fannie Mae and Mordecai having lunch. She went to them and asked, "Don't I know you from somewhere? I'm Rosemary Allison from Hattiesburg."

Recognizing her instantly, they both rose from their seats and greeted her with smiles. "You sure do know us," said Fannie Mae. "We're both from the same area, Route 5. I'm Fannie Mae Johnson, used to be Brown until I married him," pointing her thumb at Mordecai.

Mordecai grinned and said, "You sure do know me. I'm the possum hunter that used to bring possums and coons to ya'll to eat."

"Ugh," replied Rosemary. "Please don't remind me."

"You don't like possums I take it," said Fannie.

"Like it? I detest it," said Rosemary. "May I sit with ya'll?"

"You shore can," said Mordecai as he pulled up a chair for her. Although they had never formally been introduced before, they established a new friendship readily. More than once did they "hang" together, on and off campus for conversation and food. Rosemary thoroughly enjoyed the home cooked meals at their place of dwelling, especially the fried chicken.

In 1971 Rosemary graduated with a degree in finance and married Oliver Taylor of Louisville, Mississippi, who became a student of law at the University of Mississippi's School of Law. They married and

THE POSSUM HUNTER

divorced. He did not make the kind of money it took for her living standards.

Frederick Allison, Jr. was now a freshman on campus and occasionally joined in with them on their eating and conversation escapades. He and Mordecai got along fine on a level that was once forbidden—as equals, as two men, one not superior to the other. They attended athletic events together and drank beer together.

When Suzanne entered the freshman class in 1971 she had just missed socializing with Fannie Mae and Mordecai for any length of time. Occasionally when she visited her brother and sister at State, they would all team up for a bite to eat or drink. Suzanne respected them, and for the first time in her young life, had witnessed mentally talented Negroes. Fannie Mae's A+ average in higher mathematics really "blew her mind" and changed her concept of blacks as a whole. Mordecai told her that there were others just as smart or perhaps smarter than them on her father's plantation but they had not had the chance to learn. Some dropped out of school and ran away up North.

In 1971 Suzanne learned in her social studies class about the Supreme Court declaring that "objective" criteria unrelated to job skill for hiring employees were discriminatory if they put minorities at a relative disadvantage. She learned that the Court upheld bussing of school children where segregation had been an officially supported policy and no acceptable alternative had been suggested by local authorities. Also, she became aware that at New York's Attica Prison, more than one thousand black and Latino prisoners rioted over the lack of educational opportunities and that the Reverend Jesse Jackson organized PUSH, People United to Save Humanity while his brother, Chuck Jackson, sang the hit tune *Any Day Now*.

Suzanne's outlook would be changed and the world outside of Hungerville would be different. Perhaps this could explain why as she traveled the world that she very seldom saw American blacks.

* * * * *

1979, one year before DNA was established as the blueprint of heredity and could then be used to identify true parental father or mother. Mordecai was aware of its existence and it concerned him very much. What would happen if Little Willie's true father was identified as Fred or Calvin? Would Fannie forsake him for either one of them and take Little Willie with her? Would she leave Rosa with him or try to take her with her? Would Fred or Calvin want to accept Rosa as part of the deal? Would he try to hold onto his family?

Fred wrote Fannie a letter to be delivered via Dr. Calvin Lucas. Dr. Lucas requested a conference with his student, Dr. Fannie Mae Johnson. This conference had all the makings of a professional conference between two professional mathematicians. It read:

Dear Dr. Johnson:
We, the Society of Applied Advance Mathematicians, request your participation in the discussion of Eudoxus' most famous discoveries—the volume of a cone and the extension of arithmetic to the rationales, summing formula for geometric series.

The meeting will be held in the conference room adjacent to the library. Please bring your oldest offspring.

Mordecai questioned why bring the oldest offspring? He drove them to the meeting and let them out as he observed several others with their children attending. He was asked to return in two hours to pick them up, so he and Rosa rode on to the pizza parlor for a bite to eat.

Calvin had planned it well. The other people were invited to avoid suspicion. They all were dismissed after thirty minutes so that he could be alone with Little Willie and Fannie. He handed Fred's letter to Fannie and took Little Willie for a walk. He wanted to spend as much time with his prospective son as he could. They talked and discussed many issues. He gave Little Willie some mathematical problems to solve. He was now twelve years old and 10th grade. The problems he gave him were on the twelfth grade level. Little Willie solved all in a matter of minutes and smiled. That smile reminded Calvin of himself at that age. "He has

THE POSSUM HUNTER

to be my son," said Calvin to himself. He hugged him, then took him back to his mother who had just finished reading Fred's letter.

Pretty smart young man you have here, Dr. Johnson," Calvin said. "I just got through giving him some tough math problems to solve and he solved them all."

"Yes, he takes after his daddy," Fannie said. Calvin was certain she meant him.

Fred;s letter:

> Dear Fannie:
> Science is almost at the point where the true father can be determined with certainty. Are you still willing for all of us to be tested by an impartial doctor? If I'm the father, will you marry me? If you won't, then can we all acknowledge it and let me provide for him and, at times, let us spend some time together?
> Sincerely yours,
> Fred
>
> P.S. You may call or write me at the medical center or at my home in Tougaloo. Yes, I still live in Mississippi where I practice internal medicine. I go back to New York only for visits. I'm somewhat engaged to a beautiful girl whom I don't love. I love only you and will continue to do so even if the child is not mine. I pray that it is mine.
>
> Love, Fred

1979, one year before the final truth, Dr. Fred Woullard met with Dr. Calvin Lucas in his office as before to plan their strategy on how they should go about the procedure. Their biggest problem would be Mordecai. He'd have to know and give approval, wouldn't he? They would have to meet together with Fannie Mae alone first, they both agreed. Calvin would arrange this destructive meeting, and Fred would work on the biological aspect. They then tabled this issue to explore each other's minds once more. It had been nine years since their last and first parley.

The issues of their discussions would include DNA, from Friedrich Meischer of Germany in 1869 to the determination of the double-helical structure by F. H. Crick of England and James D. Watson of the United States in 1953 to the present stage. They would discuss the now president of the United States, President Jimmy Carter. Carter on June 12, 1979, offered a $18.2 billion plan for the poor and elderly.

On November 3, 1979, five people were killed in a march against Klans. Four were shot dead, the fifth fatally wounded in Greensboro, NC, as demonstrators prepared for the anti-Klan march. Ten others were injured, eight with gunshot wounds. Fourteen Ku Klux Klansmen were arraigned on November 5 on murder charges. President Carter ordered a nationwide investigation of Klan activities.

Music would be included in their conversation. In 1979 the musical *Grease* broke Broadway records (December 8) with its 3,243rd performance at the Royale Theater, breaking the mark set by *Fiddler on the Roof*.

Rhodesia won its independence as Zimbabwe with black majority rule (December 12, 1979-April 18, 1980).

They discussed other issues such as: Patty Hearst, convicted in bank robbery, was freed from a federal penitentiary under clemency (February 2, 1979). The power of the rich influence!

The Shah left Iran after years of turmoil (January 16). Muslim leader Ayatollah Ruhollah Khomeini took over.

On October 30, educator Richard Arrington, age 45, became the first black mayor of Birmingham, Alabama. 90% of white votes were cast for white candidate Frank Parson, age 38. Thirty-eight lawyers and virtually all blacks voted for Arrington.

Time, again, evaporated—like listening to a Daniel Webster speech during the 1800's. They dined again at O'Callahan's. This time Calvin permitted Fred to treat and order on his own. He did and ordered the same thing as before. "When in Rome..."

* * * * *

THE POSSUM HUNTER

Calvin, the genius, used the same scheme as before, inviting Fannie Mae and her oldest offspring to a mathematics seminar. Mordecai, although highly suspicious, agreed and followed through. He dropped Little Willie and Fannie Mae off as he did before. There were other people there with their children, also, who were invited to cover up suspicions. They were let go after one hour, then Fred entered the room. Calvin had told her beforehand that Fred would be there and why. She had given her consent.

Instead of eating at the pizza parlor, Mordecai and Rosa got an ice cream cone at "Friendly's," a northeastern ice cream franchise, and drove to the Elms Chateau-mer, at Kingscote and Rosecliff, where the 1973 film *The Great Gatsby* was filmed, then back to the conference room.

He took Rosa by the hand, led her to the door and opened it. Facing him were four pairs of shocked eyes, staring at him like he was a gorilla. Nobody spoke. Silence reigned. Mordecai, breaking the silence, spoke. "I suppose my appearance gave you all instant amnesia." He smiled at his joke. "Why was I not invited? No one spoke. "And, Fred, you mean to tell me that you came all the way from Mississippi or New York to Providence and didn't even want to talk to me, me the one who delivered your letter?" Fred dropped his head.

"And you, Calvin," he continued. "In spite of what I knew about you and my wife, I allowed myself to accept you as a friend. I permitted myself to think that anything between the two of you was all academic. Well, I suppose it is academic. One and one equals three. One man, one woman produces a child. The question is, which one male is it?"

Fannie was the first to speak. "Oh, Mordecai, I'm sorry. I should have told you the truth about this meeting." She began to cry.

"The trouble is," Mordecai continued, "I don't give a hoot who the real daddy is. Little Willie is my son, and I'm his father regardless of who impregnated the mother. Cain't you all see that I love Little Willie and will continue to rear and take care of him, even better than either of you? Even if he is your son."

Fannie Mae gasped and shouted, "No, no, please. Let's not discuss this in front of the children."

S. EARL WILSON, III

"Oh, Fannie, can't you see that Little Willie suspects or knows? His mind is too brilliant to be treated like a dummy, so too is Rosa's mind. If you leave me for either of them, or I leave you, they gonna want to know why."
Calvin spoke. "I suppose both of you are correct. Perhaps this conversation is too deep for the children at this time. The four of us as adults should discuss this together, then explain it to them. Please accept my, or our, apology, Mordecai."
After almost regaining his composure and admiring the way Mordecai conducted himself under such an egregious situation, Fred spoke, mainly to Mordecai. Whether or not Mordecai understood him is of no concern. Three, perhaps more who stood there would understand or grasp the meaning. Some people in Mordecai's situation would have reacted angrily or violently, but he kept his cool. Fred said, "You're a better man than I am, Gunga Din!" Then continued:

It was Din! Din! Din!
Ere's a begger with a bullet through is spleen;
E's chawin up the ground an e's
Kickin all around: For Gawd's
sake, git the water Gunga Din.

Din! Din! Din! Mordecai Din!
You Lazarushian-leather Gunga Din!
Tho I've belted you and flayed you,
By the livin' God that made you
You're a better man than I am,
Gunga, Mordecai Din!

"That was from Rudyard Kipling, 1865," Mordecai said, shocking the shit out of them.
He had just recently used Kipling in his teachings when suggested by his department chairman.

* * * * *

THE POSSUM HUNTER

It was Saturday morning and the house was empty said for Mordecai and Fannie Mae. Mae Helen, Ethyl Mae, Little Willie, and Rosa had all gone with Mrs. Cleopatra Booker on another cultural educational mission for more exposure to things outside of their realm. Cleo's friend, Rebecca Bernstein's son Seth, was having his Bar Mitzvah starting at the Touro Synagogue in Newport, Rhode Island and ending at a country club.

The Touro Synagogue is the oldest synagogue in America (1763). The architect was Peter Harrison. It contains the oldest Torah—the body of Jewish doctrinal literature, the Mosiac Law—in North America. It was built by Sephardic Jews exiled from Portugal and Spain. Its beauty transcends the ordinary and is majestically built. It is an architectural masterpiece whose exterior signifies Georgian style while its interior is adorned with Ionic statues representing the twelve tribes of Israel.

A Bar Mitzvah as told by my friend and author Howard Gleichenhaus, the author of the book *Colquitt*:

Traditionally, a Bar Mitzvah takes place when a Jewish boy turns thirteen. It usually happens within a month or two of the thirteenth birthday. Preparation begins about 8-12 months before. There is also a Bat Mitzvah which is the same ceremony for girls. However, that is a relative new tradition going back less than 100 years. The ceremonies are a right of passage into adulthood but not really. It is actually when the young man or woman takes on the responsibility of adulthood as a coreligionist and is expected to take part actively as an adult in the synagogue. As we all know, it is mostly symbolic and thirteen is thirteen whether Jewish, Baptist or anything else.

Most Jewish children begin learning about the religion like almost every other religion with Sunday Schools and such. Soon, by 3-4 grade they are going to afternoon Hebrew School a few times a week and learning traditional prayers, Hebrew, history, traditions, etc. At about 12 they start learning the special prayers, etc. for the ceremony. The celebrant will be expected to lead most of the service on that big day. That involves a HAFTORAH which is a commentary portion of the prayer book that changes every week. It, along with special prayer, is changed in Hebrew. The child also chants a Torah portion. The Torah (Pentateuch) is the books of Moses from the Old Testament. It starts with Genesis. One section is read ever week and it takes a full year to go through it. Whatever week the Bar Mitzvah is scheduled for determines which chapter is read. It is also chanted in ancient Hebrew (that's why prep takes a year).

The party after can be simple or elaborate and expensive. Think about a big wedding without the bride. It can involve bands, orchestras, photographers, gowns, tuxedos, lots of food and booze. It could also be a simple luncheon for a dozen or so people. In fancy suburbs like Rockland it is more often than not the big gala affair. I made a tidy sum during my years in Ctown as a photographer of these events. It would not have been strange to shoot a job for $3,000.

Gifts are mostly money although some people do give a real present but not usually.

Mrs. Booker and her group thoroughly enjoyed themselves. The people were friendly, perhaps the friendliest white people that Mae Helen and her sister ever met. The food was abundant and delicious. The music was great and they danced for the first time in their lives with white males over and over again. Both gave their telephone numbers to handsome guys who asked to see them again.

At the end of the day, Seth was declared an adult to take part in the adult procedures in the synagogue and to start his new status with $40,000 given to him by friends and relatives of his family.

Rosa and Little Willie were flabbergasted, astonished, wiser and happy. Cleo was her normal self.

* * * * *

Mordecai had purchased an old used baby grand piano for the purpose of showing it off and for both of his children to practice while taking piano lessons. He could play "by ear" some songs that he had practiced.

THE POSSUM HUNTER

He took Fannie Mae by the hand, then led her to the piano where they both sat down. "Listen, honey, I'm going to sing you a song. Listen carefully as I play, and it says exactly what I want to say and means what I want it to mean when it comes to decision making time for you.

He played *Let It Be Me* by Betty Everett and Jerry Butler. He sang softly as she held his arm:

I bless the day I found you
I want to stay around you
And so I beg you, let it be me

Don't take this heaven from one
If you must cling to someone
Now and forever, let it be me

Each time we meet, love
I find complete love
Without your sweet love
What would life be

So never leave me lonely
Tell me you love me only
And that you'll always
Let it be me

And that you'll always
Let it be me

He then cried. Fannie kissed the tears away and said, "Darling, that's one of the most heartwarming and touching things I've ever had in my life. I'm yours forever if you want." She sang sweetly with no music:

Mordecai, I'm yours till the oceans run dry
Yours till birds cease to fly.

S. EARL WILSON, III

I'm yours till the mountains crumble
I'm yours till Niagara Falls tumble
Baby, I'm yours.

They kissed. He asked, "You promise?"
"I promise! Slide down a little, please," Fannie requested of Mordecai. Fannie could really play the piano from having taking piano lessons in high school from the principal's wife, Mrs. Wilson. She played softly and sang to him, looking directly into his eyes:

Baby, I'm yours (baby, I'm yours)
And I'll be yours (yours) until the stars fall from the sky
Yours (yours) until the rivers all run dry
In other words, until I die

Baby, I'm yours (baby, I'm yours)
And I'll be yours (yours) until the sun no longer shines
Yours (yours) until the poets run out of rhyme
In other words, until the end of time

I'm gonna stay right here by your side
Do my best to keep you satisfied
Nothin' in the world can drive me away
'Cause every day, you'll hear me say

Baby, I'm yours (baby, I'm yours)
And I'll be yours (yours) until two and two is three
Yours (yours) until the mountains crumble to the sea
In other words, until eternity

Baby, I'm yours
Til the stars fall from the sky
Baby, I'm yours
Til the rivers all run dry

THE POSSUM HUNTER

In April of 1979 this led to the making of their third child called A.J.—Anthony James Johnson born December 24, 1980. Neither of them could possibly have foreseen the resuscitative adventures that lay ahead—a concatenation of events which would lead to things beyond their wildest imaginations. Yet, through her pregnancy, Fannie Mae prevailed. The name, of course, was chosen by Cleo Booker. Ethyl Mae wanted to name him Feazelle. Mrs. Booker shouted an emphatic, "NO!"

* * * * *

It was Wednesday night after Mordecai and his family returned home from attending prayer meeting when Little Willie gently knocked upon his parents' bedroom door. "Yes," they both replied.

"Mommie and Daddy," came the reply. "It's me, Little Willie. May I please come in and talk to you?"

"Um, hum, come on in."

"Tonight, during prayer meeting, Reverend Wright said something about being distressed. He said, *In my distress I cried unto the Lord, and he heard me*. He also mentioned lying lips and deceitful tongues."

"Yes," said Mordecai. That's from the Psalm 120th."

"Well, there is something going on in our lives that is very distressful to me. I am uncomfortable, slightly confused, and tremendously hurt. I feel that I am the cause of this turmoil in yours, and others, lives—like Dr. Lucas and Dr. Woullard. I feel that you both have not told me the truth and have deceived me. I think that I know what the problem is but I want to hear it from you. Do y'all love me or regret that I was born?" Little Willie began to cry and begged, "Please don't hate me!"

Fannie Mae embraced and kissed him, wiping his tears away while shedding tears of her own. "My darling baby, Mommie loves you to death and will continue to love you even unto death. I'm sorry that you are distressed, but it is Mommie's fault, not yours or Daddy's. I shall tell you the truth that you should have been told a long time ago, but I was too ashamed to tell you."

Mordecai took him into his arms, lifting him from the floor. "Little Willie," he said. "I love you more than a pig loves slop, more than a mule loves hay, more than a possum loves persimmons. I am your daddy, no matter what, and will continue to be." He too shed tears. They both laughed, as Little Willie hugged his daddy.

Fannie Mae spoke. "I'm going to tell you the truth, even if the truth might make you hate and disrespect me. When I was a young and foolish student, I was involved sexually with three men—Dr Lucas while studying at Brown University, Dr. Woullard, who was my steady date at Tougaloo. I became pregnant. One of them is your biological father, and they want to know who the real father really is. Mordecai and I were lovers since high school. We broke up at Tougaloo and came together again when Dr. Fred Lucas, after learning that I was pregnant, deserted me. Mordecai married me to give you a name and to save my honor. Now that you've heard my A, B, C's, tell me what you think of me. It is not a case of not being wanted. It's a case of too many people wanting you."

"Mommie, I can't blame you for being promiscuous during your younger days. The same holds true today. Girls are hot for me. I could have lost my virginity a long time ago—I just didn't. I feel lucky to be here. If you had used protected sex or had an abortion, I would not have been born. I thank you for life, and I thank Daddy for raising and caring for me, making me the healthy, handsome dude that I am. I love you both and even though I've never said it before, thank you very much for being my parents. The DNA doesn't mean a thing. Daddy, you will always be my father. Doesn't this all seem like a soap opera?" They all grinned.

* * * * *

May 1980—The Truth

A meeting was called for, the spring of 1980, by Dr. Fred Woullard of Jackson, Mississippi, who now felt confident that DNA testing was certain and foolproof in determining paternity. The others had read

THE POSSUM HUNTER

likewise. The person of contact would be Professor Mordecai Johnson first. If he gave his approval, the others would be notified afterwards. Mordecai approved of a meeting and suggested it be held at his house May 23, 1980 at 12:00 noon, a time when their minds were lively and aware, not early in the morning right after sleep where they may be recovering. Not late in the afternoon where their minds might be overworked or concerned about the issues they had already faced that day.

At the end of the meeting they would be served a lunch of fried chicken and lemonade prepared by Mae Helen and Ethyl Mae, who loved the cultural exposure but were homesick. They would use Rhode Island Red chicken that they had become fond of and would take some live ones (rooster and hens) back home.

At the beginning of the meeting held in the spacious living room, Mordecai spoke first. "We welcome you to our humble house." (It wasn't humble by any means—a typical New England middle class chateau.) Both Fred and Calvin were impressed. They both admired their baby grand piano, also. Mordecai continued, "If there is anything that I can do to make you more comfortable, please don't hesitate to ask me. This meeting means so much to three but very little to one, me. Nevertheless, let's get it on."

Fred spoke. "There is now a foolproof method of determining parenthood called DNA testing. This method, without doubt, can tell which of us is the true, authentic biological father. The test is harmless and painless but expensive. I propose that we all share the cost. Due to the sensitivity of the situation, I suggest choosing a place void of either one of our influence. A neutral site and a scientist who is impartial that has never seen or met either one of us. One who could care less about the outcome. Do you agree?" he asked.

They all agreed. Then Calvin asked, "How do you suggest we find this neutral site and doctor?"

"Let's first eliminate states like New York, Mississippi, Rhode Island, Alabama. Perhaps the entire Northeast," Fannie said.

Calvin then looked at Mordecai and spoke, "Mordecai, since you're the one who has the most to lose and the least to gain, why don't you be the one who makes the suggestion?"

Mordecai disgustingly replied, "I told ya'll that I don't give a damn about this shit, but I got an idea. I got a map of the whole United States in my attic and a set of darts there also. I think we should tape the map to the wall and let Fannie Mae throw a dart. Wherever it lands away from the off-limits states, that'll be it." They all laughed and agreed.

The map was taped to the kitchen's door, and Fannie Mae threw the dart that pierced the state of Tennessee right by the city of Nashville. "Anybody ever been to or got connections in Tennessee?" asked Fannie.

"I got beat up in Knoxville while serving as a Freedom Rider one time in the '60's," Mordecai answered.

"That doesn't matter," said Fred. "There is a black medical school there, Meharry, in Nashville. This may be the perfect place. If it's OK with the rest of you, I'll research the names of some staff doctors there and we can choose the man or woman."

"Anyone you select is OK," Fannie Mae said. "We will all have to go there, including Little Willie, and spend a few days there. Mordecai, why don't we drive and take Mae Helen, Ethyl Mae, and Rosa with us, too, and expose them to more of the USA?"

"All right," said Mordecai. "I've always wanted to go the Grand Ole Opry anyway." Regardless of the outcome, he harbored no fear of losing Fannie Mae. She had already said, "I do and I promise."

* * * * *

The person chosen was Dr. Henry Wendell Foster, Jr., Dean of the School of Medicine, Meharry College and Clinical Professor, Obstetrics and Gynecology, and Clinical Professor of ObGy, Vanderbilt University. Dr. Foster received his undergraduate degree from Morehouse College and his Doctor of Medicine degree from the University of Arkansas in 1958 where he was inducted into Alpha Omega Alpha National Honor Medical Society. He was the only African-American in his class of 96 students. He did his internship at

THE POSSUM HUNTER

Detroit Receiving Hospital, 1958-59, and spent two years as a medical officer in the U.S. Air Force, 1959-61. Upon his discharge, he was a resident physician in general surgery in Malden, Massachusetts, 1961-62, and completed a residency in obstetrics and gynecology at Meharry Medical College, 1962-65.

Upon finishing his postgraduate training, Dr. Foster assumed the position of Chief of Obstetrics and Gynecology at the John A. Andrew Memorial Hospital of Tuskegee University (formerly Tuskegee Institute). While at Tuskegee, he helped pioneer what has become a national model for regionalized perinatal health care systems throughout the country. It was primarily this activity that led to his induction into the Institute of Medicine of the National Academy of Sciences in 1972 as one of its youngest inductees ever. While serving as Professor and Chairman of Meharry's Department of Obstetrics and Gynecology, Dr. Foster spent five years as Senior Program Consultant for the Robert Wood Johnson Foundation and directed its Program to Consolidate Health Services for High-Risk Young People, 1981-86.

From this program he conceptualized and developed the "I Have A Future Program," to reduce teen pregnancy, which was recognized by President George Bush in 1991, as one of the nation's "Thousand Points of Light."

During his career, Dr. Foster has produced more than 250 publications and abstracts as well as contributed chapters to textbooks, has written a book, *Make A Difference*, and has developed audiovisual educational materials. He has conducted 80 formal university lectureships and his professional expertise has been sought across the globe. He has participated in conferences, seminars, and hearings in Spain, Mexico, Peru, Kenya, South Africa, Egypt, Mainland China, Canada, Singapore, Vietnam, the United Kingdom, Australia, Russia, Nigeria, India, Bangladesh and Cuba.

* * * * *

Mordecai and his entourage of Ethyl Mae, Mae Helen, Little Willie, Rosa, and Fannie Mae arrived in Nashville Sunday morning by station wagon. Both Fred and Calvin flew and missed the beautiful scenery and stops. Their first stop was New Haven, Connecticut, where they visited the Convention and Visitors Bureau, 195 Church Street, settled by Puritans in 1638. The town still maintains its original village green, a 16 acre square bordered by three churches and Yale University. Then onwards to New York where they saw their first Broadway play, the Statue of Liberty, and the Empire State Building. From New York to Atlantic City, New Jersey where they drank soda, ate salt water taffy and hot dogs, and swam. From there to Philadelphia where they saw the Benjamin Franklin National Memorial and Home. While there they also took in the Afro-American Historical and Cultural Museum on 7th and Arch Streets. From Philadelphia onwards to Baltimore, Maryland, where they visited the Great Blacks in Wax Museum at 1601 East North Avenue where Afro-American history is the focus. There are more than 100 life sized wax figures representing people who influenced events in ancient Africa, the Civil War, the Harlem Renaissance, as well as modern civil rights leaders. They also visited the Star-Spangled Banner House

THE POSSUM HUNTER

and 1812 Museum, 844 East Pratt Street. This is the home of the woman who sewed the flag that inspired Francis Scott Key to write the *National Anthem*.

Onwards to the Nation's Capitol, Washington, DC, to the Lincoln Memorial, to the White House, to the Capitol to the stories of Benjamin Banneker, the black genius, mathematician, and surveyor, who built a wooden clock that kept accurate time for 50 years who designed the city of Washington, DC.

This journey of 15 days took them through Virginia, West Virginia, across the Appalachian Mountains into Tennessee. They arrived happy but exhausted.

Mordecai knew that the revealing of the truth would hurt and bother him tremendously but he would survive unless Fannie Mae changed her mind. His lifelong dream of visiting the Grand Ole Opry could now be fulfilled. Maybe he would see some of his heroes in person. Person such as Minnie Pearl, Grandpa Jones, Dolly Parton, Loretta Lynn, or George Jones. Perhaps Minnie Pearl could make him laugh along with "Hee Haw."

* * * * *

The adults, Fannie Mae, Calvin Lucas, Fred Woullard, and Mordecai all met with Dr. Foster in his conference room.

Dr. Foster spoke. "From the information already given to me by Dr. Fred Woullard, I have a precognition of the issues that confront us, however, I would like it told again by the mother of the offspring."

Fannie Mae recapitulated the story already told by Fred but poignantly so. With tears in her eyes, she retold the story from the beginning till the presence and ending her anecdote by saying, "Oh, Doctor Foster, I suppose you think of me as an immoral, disreputable, sinful person."

Foster replied, "My dear Mrs. Johnson, I am not God. I don't have the authority or power to judge. To me you are a decent human being who gave birth. An abortion would have negated all of this, but you chose the opposite, thank God, and a brilliant child was born. Whatever the truth reveals, you are strong enough to handle it. Any black Mississippi gal who is smart enough to get her Ph.D. in math from Brown is truly no weakling nor prude. Your pillar of strength is your trust in God, and your husband, who like Ben E. King sings, is willing, regardless of the outcome, to *Stand by You.*"

"That's the truth." said Mordecai.

Dr Foster said, "What I want is, tomorrow morning at 8:00 a.m., for all of you plus the child to meet me at the clinic for the first stage of the testing. Then give me three days to draw a positive conclusion. We shall also send to Vanderbilt samples to be tested. If both our results coincide, we will have all the proof we need for a positive identification. If not we start all over again working together at the same site, either here or there."

The Next Day

The next day, as Mordecai drove Little Willie and Fannie Mae to the clinic, he was asked to stay and be tested also.

"What's the sense in me being tested, Doctor?" he asked Doctor Foster.

"Well, I don't want to leave any stones uncovered or leave out any remote possibilities. Besides, we can use you as a "control." (A control is a standard of comparison for testing the result of a scientific experiment.)

Mordecai grinned and submitted. Foster said as he and his assistant began the process. "It is ideal for the men, woman, and child to give DNA, but it is 99% accurate even if the mother does not participate. A 100% would require the DNA of every man on planet Earth."

DNA is obtained by using hair strands or a mouth swab. In this case both methods would be applied.

Hair strands were taken from each participant, and buccal swabs were collected. (Buccal swab collection: samples for a DNA test, such as a paternity test, are routinely collected using the painless and simple buccal swab—similar to a cotton-tipped swab, but made of the special material Dacron. The swab is rubbed against the inside cheek of the test participant, and loose cheek cells adhere to the swab. Unlike regular cotton swabs, Dacron provides a consistent surface for sample collection and DNA extraction.)

The samples collected are sent to the laboratory in a sealed, tamper-evidence package. Each sample is recored and the DNA test begins. There are five steps:

1. Samples from each person are divided in two for Dual Process. From this point on, two independent laboratory teams take the samples through the DNA testing process.
2. DNA is extracted from the buccal swabs and purified.
3. The extracted DNA is added to a special chemical mix for the Polymerase Chain Reaction (PCR), a process that targets 16 specific locations in the DNA (called loci) and makes billions of copies of each location.
4. The products of PCR are analyzed to create a DNA profile, a genetic equivalent of a fingerprint for each tested party.
5. The child's DNA profile is compared with the alleged father's and statistical analysis is performed to determine the probability of paternity. A 0% probability of paternity represents an exclusion.

Two of the things that intrigued Dr. Calvin Lucas the most were, like him, he was a Morehouse college graduate and both had "crossed the burning sands" into Pi Chapter of Kappa Alpha Psi Fraternity. Dr. Fred Woullard was thoroughly impressed with Foster's credentials but apathetic about his Greek membership because Fred himself was a member of the Alpha Phi Alpha fraternity.

Dr. Fannie Mae Johnson was thoroughly impressed with Dr. Foster's dignity, accomplishments, wisdom, and knowledge and the way he treated her as though she had done no wrong.

Dr. Foster's military experience and rank impressed Mordecai the most. He seemed to have the "air" of an *Officer and a Gentleman*. During his time in the Marine Corps, Mordecai had seen only three black officers, the one who pulled him into the helicopter when he was shot in the leg, a warrant officer at Quantico Marine Base, and a young lieutenant that was killed in Viet Nam. Mordecai liked him so much that made him wonder if Foster ate possum, too.

* * * * *

During the three day waiting period, they all joined together in visiting Tennessee State University, Fisk University, and Vanderbilt. With the persuasion of Mordecai, they all went to the Grand Ole Opry where they all saw Little Jimmie Dickens, Porter Wagoner, Merle Haggard,

THE POSSUM HUNTER

Charley Pride, and Willie Nelson. All, except Fred, were familiar with country music and enjoyed it. Fred, after seeing Charley Pride, kinda felt more comfortable and enjoyed the rest of the show. And if this wasn't enough, they visited Twitty City, the home of country music star Conway Twitty (who originally was from Mississippi) at 1 Music City Blvd. in Hendersonville, and the House of Cash, too, on Johnny Cash Parkway.

Dr. Foster had recommended several great restaurants to satisfy both their taste and curiosities. They found his recommendations excellent choices and ate like they had never been fed before.

On the third day, the day of rectitude and truth, they all, except Little Willie, met in the office of Dr. Henry Foster. He served them coffee, tea, soft carbonated drinks, or alcohol, if they desired. Also a tray of hor d'oeurves.

"I have the results," he said. "The truth is astoundingly bizarre, uncanny but perhaps wonderful." The silence of the listeners was dramatically prevalent. "Dr. Lucas and Dr. Woullard, neither of you is the biological father," spoke Foster. "Mordecai, the test shows that you are 99.99% the true biological father!"

"How can this be?" asked Dr. Lucas.

"You forgot to do your math, Professor," Dr. Foster responded. "The period of gestation in human beings is nine months. The child was born in February 1967. You both had sex with the mother in May. If it were either of you, then the baby would have been born in January. Mordecai had to have had intercourse in May and June. But regardless, DNA does not lie. For whatever the reason, Mordecai is the true father."

Mordecai, although shocked incredibly, smiled from ear to ear. "Are you sure, Doctor Foster?" Mordecai asked.

"I'm sure," he replied.

"But I was pregnant in May," Fannie Mae replied.

"No, you were not. You only thought you were. You perhaps had a condition called pseudocyesis, where a woman misses her period emanating from a psychological genesis causing an intense desire to be pregnant but where she believes she's pregnant but really is not. Hence, it is characterized as a false pregnancy. Pseudocyesis can cause many of the signs and symptoms associated with pregnancy and can resemble the condition in every way except for fetal presence. The symptoms of phantom pregnancy are similar to the symptoms of true pregnancy and are difficult to distinguish. Amenorrhoea, morning sickness, tender breasts, and gaining weight can all happen with false pregnancy."

"Is this something unique and new, Doctor Foster?" asked Fred.

"Unique, yes," answered Foster. "New? No. Hippocrates wrote about it in or around 300 B.C. when he recorded 12 different cases. Mary Tudor, Queen of England, in the 1500s, believed more than once that she was pregnant and was not. Some say that she was so upset that it made her react violently, thereby earning her the nickname "Bloody Mary," to be a reaction to her disappointment of realizing she was not pregnant."

The two great minds of Dr. Fred Woullard and Dr. Calvin Lucas became fascinated with the mind of Dr. Henry Foster. They would stick around a few days longer where they would eat and have discourse with him. His mind was as great or greater than theirs. Calvin was especially intrigued with Foster. They both were "Morehouse Men."

Mordecai grabbed Fannie Mae, hugged her, danced, and shook everybody's hand. He then took some of Dr. Foster's scotch, poured himself, and everybody else a drink and proposed a toast.

"Here's to the son, even though I thought he was not mine, but treated him and accepted him as mine, was really mine anyway." They all clinked their glasses together, exhaled and swallowed.

Although disappointed at not being the true father, Fred breathed a sigh of relief. His conscious was now clear and he could now marry Gizelle. As beautiful as she was and as handsome as he was, Fred thought, "We can make our own children, and they will be beautiful and smart."

Calvin had not really loved Fannie Mae as did Fred and Mordecai but was intrigued and fascinated over her. He had thought about asking her to marry him if the child were his, but the revelation that he was not, lifted a burden from his shoulders, leaving him free to now marry Dr.

THE POSSUM HUNTER

Loren Hunter, And, yes, he would take her home to Birmingham. To hell with those rednecks and nigs.

Dr. Foster then handed his bill to them—$6,000. Fannie, Fred, and Calvin each paid $2,000.

Reactions

When Little Willie was told who his real daddy was, he embraced Mordecai and cried, saying, "Thank you, Lord. Thank you, Jesus."

Rosa didn't know what was going on so she had no reason to react.

Mae Helen and Ethyl Mae screamed out loud and hugged and kissed their brother-in-law. They then called home to break the news to their family.

Lonzo said, "Huh, you ain't telling me nothing that I didn't already know. They shudda listen to me and saved all that money. I told you in the beginning that they feets is too much alike."

Fannie Mae was flabbergasted and surprised but amazed also. What a wonderful and amazing man she had married; a man who not only rescued her from shame, endured her hardship, pain and sorrow, lost a limb on account of her, lifted them both from poverty to middle class, traded the country for town so that she could pursue her dreams of becoming a Ph.D., giving up possums for lobsters, and when threatening to lose her, begged her to stay with him. My, what a man!

"I love you, Mordecai, more today than yesterday. You are my man, a mountain of a man!"

"I love you, too, Fannie Mae, and I'm glad that you stayed with me. Those two, Fred and Calvin, are mighty nice fellows but they were barking up the wrong tree. They were like coon dogs hunting rabbits."

Back Home Again

From Nashville they, Mordecai and company, would go to Hungerville, Mississippi outside of Hattiesburg. They would, in a sense, be going back home. There had been so many changes in Mordecai's

THE POSSUM HUNTER

and Fannie Mae's lives, also Mae Helen's and Ethyl Mae's lives now, that it would seem unrealistic or bizarre to refer to home as being located in the rural elements of Hattiesburg's Forrest County and Lamar, Perry, and Jones Counties. Not the elegance of New England—dining on quahogs and shrimp instead of chitterlings and rice, lobsters in place of raccoons and gravy; gazing up at skyscrapers instead of the tallest pine trees; looking at the Atlantic Ocean instead of Leaf River; fishing in the Narraganset Bay as opposed to fishing in the Paul B. Johnson Lake.

Time had made blatant changes in their lives, but not too many "back home," or "Down South" as they and many others who had left referred to it as.

As they drove from Nashville, Tennessee in their brand new 1980 Chevy station wagon, their conversation drifted back to the sixties when they first experienced life outside of Hungerville. Their journey would take them from Nashville to Chattanooga, through Huntsville, Birmingham, and Tuscaloosa, Alabama, where they would spend the night and explore the teaching opportunities at the University of Alabama and Stillman College. From Tuscaloosa to Meridian, Mississippi to home before darkness. They would spend the rest of the summer there. Mae Helen and Ethyl Mae had almost completed their requirements to become Rhode Island certified teachers. They would decide whether to remain at home and teach or to follow Mordecai and Fannie Mae back to Providence. There would be about a ten thousand dollar difference in salary. In Forrest and surrounding counties in Mississippi, they would earn perhaps five to six thousand dollars a year. In Providence, they could earn at least fifteen thousand plus compensation for extra duties and events. What would you do?

Their Conversations

During the sixties in Hungerville, Mississippi, it was business as usual with a few minor changes. To America in general, drastic changes were exploding and widening her horizons. In 1960, television color was mastered, and people began to switch from black and white to color television. Most people in Hungerville didn't even have televisions.

Some had radios when transistors were invented but didn't bother to get one or switch when they could have heard the introduction of rock and roll music and listen to artists like Big Brother and the Holding Company along with Janis Joplin singing *Mercedes Benz* and *Me and Bobby McGee* from her album Pearl listed by *Rolling Stone Magazine* as Number 122 of the 500 greatest albums of all times. No, in Hungerville they still listened to "Randy Records" of WLAC of Tennessee and country music on WFOR in Hattiesburg, Mississippi.

In 1964 Bell Telephone revolutionized the way we make telephone calls by introducing touch tone instead of dialing. This affected perhaps a dozen people in Hungerville.

When Neil Armstrong walked on the moon in 1969 and uttered these words

One small step for man, one giant leap for mankind

Nobody, except the Allisons and a few others, saw, heard, or believed it. An enigma, words spoken in riddles—something hard to understand or believe.

Most missed the debut of Johnny Carson, the king of the *Tonight Show*, in 1962, and the Beatles in 1964 singing *I Want to Hold Your Hand*.

THE POSSUM HUNTER

If they could have heard the Rolling Stones in 1965 singing *I Can't Get No Satisfaction*, they would have said, "Me neither."

Fortunately, they missed the hippie culture with free love, hallucinating drugs, pot, and Woodstock along with the "summer of love" in San Francisco. In 1969 they had no knowledge of thousands of young people around the country going to San Francisco, California, wearing flowers in their hair, a reference to Scott McKenzie's version of the John Phillips' song *San Francisco*, an ubiquitous hit and a hippie's theme song.

Some of the folks were not entirely cheated because they listened to and danced to music played on radio station WLAC. In 1963 they heard Jackie Wilson's *Baby Work Out*, Ray Charles' *Busted* and *Don't Set Me Free*, Martha and the Vandelles' *Heatwave*, and the Impressions' *It's All Right*. In 1963 they heard *Ain't Nothing You Can Do* by Bobby Blue Bland, *Baby Love* by the Supremes, *Let It Be Me* by Bettye Everett and Jerry Butler. Those who listened to country music were treated to the angelic and melodious voice of Patsy Cline singing *Faded Love*. Almost all people in Hungerville were doing the "Twist" and knew Chubby Checker.

When Lee Iacocca and the Ford Motor Company revolutionized the automobile industry by introducing the Mustang, Hungerville was not left out because Thomas Allison, Jr. owned and drove one. There was no envy or jealousy because their minds were trained to think that the boss's son was supposed to ride in style, not in buggies, wagons, ground slides, or used cars and pickup trucks like them.

* * * * *

On the front corner, just to the left of the road on Fannie Mae's lot, stood their place of stay. Their home away from home, their trailer that they had purchased while students at Mississippi State. Mordecai's father, Oscar, had secured it with a solid foundation, added an extra room, and built a fence enclosing it. Sally T. kept it spotless. There was food stocked in the freezer, and an abundance of canned goods, including preserves, on the pantry shelves. When Sally T. and her husband Oscar knew in advance that they were coming, they would fill the refrigerator with fresh items of food such as bacon, eggs, light bread, butter, mayonnaise, lettuce, tomatoes, ham, and possum and greens. They had all of the utilities—electricity, phones, cable television, gas, running water, and a cesspool to accommodate the toilets. These they kept running all year long. This is where they stayed whenever they came back home.

There had been many talks of tearing it down and building a gigantic home for retirement but Mordecai had another dream, or vision. There was a piece of land down by the lower forties on the Allison's plantation that intrigued him to the utmost. It was sixteen acres of unspoiled beauty. In the spring, summer, and autumn the grass was as green as the green grass of Lochmormond. The soil beneath was as fertile as the lands of the Delta. Untouched by man for years, flowers bloomed in abundance as did berries, mayhaws and pecan trees. Around a very old dilapidated, two-story house that hadn't been lived in since anybody knew or could recall, not even Aunt Minnie, the oldest person in Hungerville, stood three majestic oaks whose limbs covered with moss appeared as beautiful, giant canopies. Their roots were firmly embedded in the earth and have withstood many storms, even hurricanes. On the lower end was a medium-sized pond, or lake, teeming with fish. Mordecai, Fannie Mae, and others had fished there more than once, and their catches were bountiful.

Mordecai had written, called, and talked to Mr. Allison about purchasing this property. Mr. Allison politely refused on grounds that this was property that had been in the family for generations and would only be sold or given to family members only. Thus far, no one had expressed a desire to own it for themselves. "Perhaps one day a grand or great-grandchild will choose to own and restore the gallant old mansion and bring new life once again."

It was the middle of July, that Friday evening, as Mordecai, his family, and Alonzo sat outside on the porch talking and drinking Coca Colas when they saw the headlights of a sedan approaching their trailer. "I wonder who dat can be?" said Alonzo.

"Must be somebody white," said Fannie. "Ain't many colored folks around here got cars like that."

THE POSSUM HUNTER

Fannie was correct. It was Thomas Allison driving his Mercedes Benz by himself. He stopped, got out of the car, took off his hat, and spoke. "Good evening, everybody. May I come in?"

"You surely can, Mr. Allison," Mordecai said. "Care for a bit of possum and a Coke? We just got through eating some and have quite a bit left. My little girl here don't like possum just like your little girl didn't either."

"Don't mind if I do. Sure it won't be too much trouble?" asked Thomas.

"No, not at all," said Fannie Mae. "Rosa, fix Mr. Allison a plate. Come on in, sir, and have a seat at the table."

"Oh, mommy," Rosa whined, "do I have to? It's bad enough forcing me to taste and eat a piece."

Thomas Allison laughed and then cried. "She reminds me so much of my younger daughter Suzanne whom I've lost and may never see again. Oh, God, no!" he cried.

"What's the matter, Mr. Allison? What do you mean you may never see her again?" asked Mordecai.

"That's why I came here, to talk to you. You are my last hope or resort."

"Eat. Eat your possum now and talk when you finish," Fannie interrupted. Thomas ate as though it was his last meal as Rosa watched in horror.

When he finished he said, "Thank you. Mighty good possum, mighty good." He drank his Coca Cola, wiped his mouth, lit his Camel cigarette, inhaled, and began his conversation. "You see, y'all, Suzanne, after finishing Mississippi State, took up with and began dating a young single professor, Dr. Herman Joyce, from the state of Nebraska who had just gotten his Ph.D. from State also. In 1976 they became engaged but did not marry. They, against our will, lived together. He insisted that he could not marry her unless she became a member of his religion which is no more than a cult."

"I cannot, for the sake of me, see how intelligent human beings can believe in things like Scientology or cults. In order to join, one has to attend training schools, then step by step move up the ladder until graduation is given or earned. The first step costs four thousand dollars, the second step is twelve thousand dollars, and graduation is only fifteen hundred, which now seems like a bargain. Then they are allowed to find jobs or given tasks to do on their own compounds. Dr. Joyce taught philosophy and literature at the University of Nebraska while Suzanne was given the job as a recruiter—getting and encouraging people to pay for the "Three Steps of Purity." Ninety percent of each of their earnings go to the religion leader—"Xanthus, the Immortal Horse."

"Their minds have been so distorted and twisted that they believe material things and wealth are sinful and should only be enjoyed by their God and leader Xanthus. They believe that their lives began on the planet Venus and that they all will return there sometime in the near future. Their leader will provide them with the money he collects from them. Suzanne is so brainwashed that she denies us as being her real parents and says her true parents are on Venus awaiting her return."

"First, we went there and tried to convince her to return with us. She would not. Next, we took our lawyer, preacher, and the police with us. She still refused and the police nor lawyer could do nothing as long as it was her own free will. She was unkempt, dirty, and drugged, it seemed. The next time we tried brute force. I took with me weapons, guns, and two bounty hunters and hoodlums. We all were all overwhelmed, beaten and defeated. Our weapons were taken, our vehicles confiscated, and our shoes taken. We were made to walk outside the gate. You have to enter and leave through the gate because the wall which surrounds the compound is twenty feet high with razor-like blades or glass plus steel-pointed metal across the top with electrical shocks. But even before one who would attempt there is an alarm system surrounding the whole area."

Thomas said, "Mordecai, I don't blame you if you curse me out and throw me from your land and house for what I'm about to ask you. But your being an ex-Marine who earned medals for rescuing people in the Viet Nam War would be the likely candidate who could succeed where all of us have failed. Will you rescue my baby? Can it be done?"

"Mr. Allison, I'm not going to throw you out of my house. I'm not going to give you my answer tonight cause I need to think. We'll meet

THE POSSUM HUNTER

tomorrow night at your house. These things I'll need if you have them: a map of the area including all roads to and from towns or places fifteen to twenty-five miles away; major highways; railroad and train schedules, both passenger and freight. How much money are you willing to spend on expenses?"

"The sky is the limit, Mordecai," Thomas replied. "A million or more, if necessary, including your price."

"If I do it, I won't charge you one dime. I'll do it for the sake of God and Suzanne. If I succeed, I'll ask you only one small favor."

"Anything, anything within my power," Thomas cried. "What time tomorrow?" he asked.

"Round 8:00, ok?"

"Round 8:00," Thomas said as he left. "If you decline, I won't blame you. And another thing I forgot to mention. Suzanne took with her our housekeeper's daughter, Pattie Sue Garrison, whom she thought she owed for us holding them in slavery. Her mission was to free her mind, body, and soul. Pattie Sue followed her willingly as a pup follows his master. Her mind too has become distorted, and she is also faithful to "Xanthus." She is one of his three female "robot-like" servants or messengers. They light his cigarettes and catch the ashes. They help him out of his bed in the morning, bathe him, dress him, scrub his office each day for purity's sake. They see to it that he is well fed, escort him to the bathroom, wipe his ass, and put him to bed at night. For this, they are promised a place of high echelon in their new home on Venus. She, too, needs to be rescued."

When Thomas Allison drove away, Fannie Mae spoke. "I feel sorry for him and his family, but, darling, you ain't serious about this rescuing mission, are you?"

"I don't quite know. It does seem quite exciting and intriguing for an ex-Marine like me. If I do, I'll need the company and help of you and Alonzo."

"What?" they both said.

"Alonzo, I'll need your strength and running ability. I'll teach you how to fight the way I learned in the Marines. Fannie Mae, I will need your driving ability and counseling service the way you did to change me back to a decent human being."

"Hmm," they both said.

Mordecai studied these diagrams completely, then decided that the rescue could be done and he would attempt it.

These are the things he required of Mr. Allison in the initial stage: a four-door Jeep station wagon with four-wheel drive, eight pair of handcuffs, five thousand dollars cash from 100s to one dollar bills plus some loose change. On their journey they would not use credit cards or checks so that their identities could not be traced. Mordecai also requested face towels and one-half gallon of chloroform $CHCl_3$, two small pistols just in case, and a private helicopter with the capacity of carrying six passengers plus the pilot.

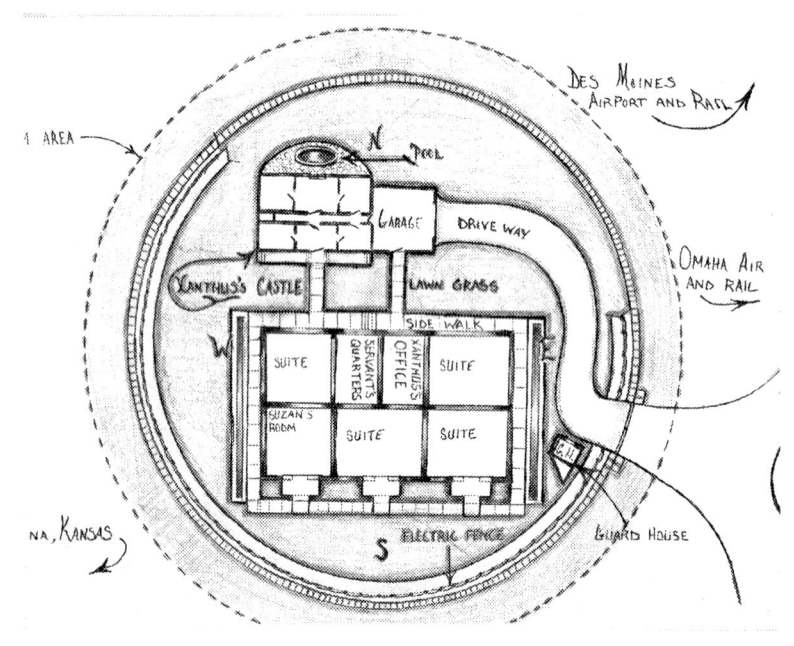

Xanthus's Compound

Mordecai's Ingenious Plans

He would hurriedly train Alonzo in Marine fighting rescue tactics and instruct him to use the .22 pistol as a last resort only, then shoot the enemy in the foot. Do not kill! Fannie Mae would begin jogging and exercising. They, along with his dad, Oscar, would build a 20 foot wall and practice throwing a hooked rope on top, then climbing to the top where they would place a thick, sturdy rubber blanket over it. This would allow them to cross over without injury or shock. They would use another rope to descend to the ground inside. Once inside, they would both engage the guards, conquer them, then place a towel filled with chlorophyll over their faces, rendering them unconscious, then proceed to the main building with the keys taken from the guards to capture their friends, Suzanne and Patty Sue. Use the word *capture*, not *rescue*, because the victims did not wish to be rescued and would probably resist or fight, requiring the use of more chlorophyll. This should not be too taxing for two strong men of their caliber—rendering them helpless and carrying them to the spot where the helicopter would pick all of them up.

August 1, 1980—Fannie Mae, Alonzo, and Mordecai, equipped with all the stuff Mordecai had requested plus more, arrived outside of Des Moines, Iowa, in a wooded area where they met Mike Anderson, the helicopter pilot who rescued Mordecai in Viet Nam. Mr. Allison had done his research and made his contact. Mordecai and Mike embraced and smiled. "Good to see you again, Sergeant Johnson. Good to see you walking," Mike said.

"I manage, thanks to you and thanks to God," replied Mordecai.

"I know all about the mission and I believe in it and endorse it. A good friend of mine lost a 20 year old daughter to them. They would not let her go so she committed suicide, threw herself into the river and drowned."

"Too bad," replied Mordecai. "Perhaps we can prevent two more."

Mordecai, going over the plans, said, "Too bad we couldn't have practiced this, but we didn't practice in 'Nam either." Spreading the map on the table he said, "Officer Anderson, we want you to drop Alonzo and myself off at this spot—a neutral spot between their alarm and detection system, a few yards from the wall. You will not land but lower us by rope to the ground, then speed away and await our signal to return inside the complex at this spot in the front of the main building. Just as in wartime, be prepared to spread the area with smoke and tear gas in case they should try to shoot at us or try to intervene. Then fly us all back to this spot in Des Moines. Leave us and take off."

* * * * *

The night of August 3, 1980, 10:00 p.m., the rescue mission began with Mordecai, Alonzo, and Mike Anderson flying to the designated spot. The people inside were concerned about the sound of a helicopter and went to view but saw nothing as Mike quickly sped away. Mordecai and Alonzo waited an hour before taking their next step. Climbing, crossing over, and descending were no problems. Crawling like snakes, they took their places in a wooded area about fifty feet from the main building. There, about five feet in front of them, they set fire to a commercial fire log, let it really catch fire, then made sounds like animals. Both the guards ran to the sight with their guns drawn. Alonzo threw a rock in the other direction and, as they turned to look, they were hit on their heads by blunt instruments of Mordecai's choosing and their faces covered with chlorophyll towels. The guards were "out like a light."

This was too easy, Alonzo thought.

With the keys taken from the guards, they opened the door to the main building. Alonzo and Mordecai, as planned, went to their

THE POSSUM HUNTER

designated areas: Mordecai to rescue Suzanne and Alonzo to get Patty Sue. They both resisted but were overcome with chlorophyll. Both carried their victims with ease.

With the signal already received by Mike Anderson, he began his return. As they walked outside for the helicopter, the alarm went off inside the building. Mordecai did not know that an deactivating code must be entered after entering the building with a key. Then the guards inside, who were not accustomed to this happening, awoke and ran to the door, catching them both. Mordecai easily defeated his encounterer with his Marine fighting skills and placed the towel over his face. Alonzo was knocked for a loop and as his assaulter straddled Alonzo, Mordecai held back his arm and applied the chlorophyll to his face. "Lights out again!"

The helicopter landed and they all boarded her. Shots were fired and Mike released smoke, tear gas, and fog in all directions, rendering anyone in the vicinity with tears, coughs, and skin-burning sensations. The helicopter ascended and went on its way. Never before had the cult confronted such a formidable force. They would in the future prepare, but, as for now, it had lost two of its members (or slaves).

Mike dropped his passengers off in the spot outside of Des Moines, then sped off. "Vaya con dios," he spoke. "May God go with you." They all loaded into the Jeep and took off with Fannie Mae as the driver.

Suzanne and Patty Sue, after regaining consciousness, began to scream and yell. "What is this? Where are we? Who are you? Why are you doing this to us?"

"We are your friends who have come to release you from bondage and free your minds. You already know us. I am Fannie Mae Brown Jackson. These two men are Mordecai Johnson and my brother Alonzo Brown. We are all from Hungerville. So quit your yelling and screaming. You are in good and safe hands. No harm will be done to you."

"Why have you captured us from our lord Xanthus?"

"Xanthus is no lord, believe me. He is an uncommon crook who doesn't use guns to rob you but uses words to rob you of your lives and true honor. He controls your minds and makes you think as he wants you to think. Why is it that he has everything and you have nothing? When

Jesus Christ walked the earth, did he dress or live better than his disciples?"

They began to think, perhaps for the first time in years. "I am hungry and thirsty," Suzanne said. "And why are my feet tied and my hands cuffed?"

"Me too," said Patty Sue.

"Your handcuffs will be removed while you eat but will be put back on when you are through eating."

"Why?"

"Why?" Because we can't trust you right now. You are still loyal to Xanthus and may attempt to return to him who is the devil himself."

"How dare you speak of our lord in such a manner?" asked Patty Sue.

"Because you are fools and can't see him for what he really is, a con artist that controls people's minds and uses them like animals and slaves. Patty Sue, if Abraham Lincoln or Martin Luther King could see you now, they would both cry and say my living has been in vain." Patty Sue began to think again.

They were fed bologna sandwiches with lettuce, tomato, and mayonnaise, with a piece of Southern fried chicken, Oreo cookies, and an iced cold Coca Cola. They ate as though they had never eaten this before. It really had been years since they had eaten anything like this.

Their diet had been one of a vegetarian's with an occasional meal of fish with only tea, water, or coffee to drink. Xanthus ate prime rib.

Fannie drove until she was completely exhausted, crossing Iowa into Illinois. It was just about daybreak that Fannie Mae pulled into a Motel Six in Aurora, Illinois. Mordecai secured two rooms adjacent to each other downstairs outside. They transferred their passengers to rooms 108 and 110. Pattie Sue and Suzanne were still chained and had to be carried inside, concealed under a blanket. Luckily, no one was up and stirring at that time in the morning. At daylight, Fannie Mae ordered room service breakfast for all of them. They showered, brushed their teeth, combed their hair, and slept. The good part about this trip for Alonzo was helping the prisoners in taking a bath or shower. They still could not be trusted to be alone. They paid him no attention for they

THE POSSUM HUNTER

were accustomed to being naked around men who could not touch them unless given permission by Xanthus. Only he had the privilege to do with them as he wished.

At night around 8:00 p.m. they checked out of the motel and drove ten hours to Pennsylvania. There they spent the morning in Harrisburg and followed the same routine as before. They continued this same sequence from Pennsylvania, through New York into Rhode Island. Fannie Mae deprogrammed their minds each day.

As agreed, there would be no communication between families until Fannie Mae initiated it. This way the shrewd and intelligent network of the cult that was capable of intercepting mail, phone calls, and people would not be alerted. Soon they would be able to listen in on the Allison's' phone and would secretly place listening devices several places in their house and cars. The Allisons had been instructed not to talk about their daughter and house servant at all. When forced to, they were instructed to be extra careful in what they said. In due time, Alonzo would fly from Chicago to Jackson, Mississippi, then catch a ride on the Greyhound bus to Hattiesburg. If they traced him, it would only lead back to Chicago.

They followed the same sequence of traveling by night and sleeping by day throughout the Midwest to the east coast with Fannie continuing her verbal assaults on cults and their leaders. She showed no mercy, calling them fools and idiots who would not use the God-given minds they were given to think, to reason, to recognize the truth. Little by little, it began to sink in. There were no drugs here, no LSD, no pot or cigarettes. Nothing but soft drinks, food, milk, water, music, fresh air, sunshine, moonlight, stars, highways, trees, cornfields, lakes, green grass, and the company of people who loved them.

At times they left before darkness so that the beauty of the states could be observed.

In Connecticut, along the seashore, Patty Sue and Suzanne were freed of their cuffs and ropes and allowed to roam and smell the air.

In Rhode Island they were taken to Mrs. Booker to live. She was given $1,500 cash for her caring for the two "lost souls." They fell instantly in love with her and her food and she with them, too. Cleo guided them, watched them, watched over them, and shared her deprogramming of them with an elderly preacher and professor from Brown University who was declared an expert in this field. Ph.D, or Doctor, Malcolm Simms came to them every Monday and they listened to him preach each Sunday.

* * * * *

The Sunday in October that Alonzo flew from Chicago to Jackson was the Sunday that both Patty Sue and Suzanne declared themselves freed from the hands and mind of Xanthus and gave themselves to Christ. This they confessed verbally aloud in Malcolm Simms' Anglican Church. They were now ready to go home and face the world on their own terms.

Alonzo, after arriving home that Sunday night, went to Thomas Allison's house. He knocked upon the door and Thelma Louise, Patty Sue's mother, let him enter from the front door. Thomas rose from his seat and embraced Alonzo. Alonzo spoke, "Mr. Allison, let's take a walk, please." They both walked out the back door into the woods where no one could listen in. They sat on a fallen tree and Alonzo told the rescue story from beginning to present. He ended by saying, "Before long Mordecai and Fannie Mae will bring them home."

Without any reservations Thomas Allison, a full grown man, cried like a baby. He then fell to his knees and cried, "Thank you, Lord." He arose, embraced Alonzo, and said, "Thank you, my friend for life, Alonzo." Alonzo was prouder than a peacock to be considered a friend of Mr. Thomas Allison. This could bring many rewards.

* * * * *

Mae Helen and Ethyl Mae had both decided to return to Rhode Island to teach. They still lived with Mordecai and Fannie Mae but were now charged for room and board. The three hundred dollars each a month was the best bargain in Providence. Most apartments went for six hundred to eight hundred a month plus utilities and food, and man,

THE POSSUM HUNTER

they could eat up a storm! However, their Jewish boyfriends took them out to eat often. But with them, they were somewhat limited. Like Jack Sprat, they could eat no fat (pork).

The six of them—Ethyl Mae, Suzanne, Fannie Mae, Mordecai, Mae Helen, Patty Sue—would ride home that Thanksgiving in the new Jeep that Thomas Allison had purchased. They would give it back to him and fly back to Providence. Even though schools frown on these actions, all school teachers took extra days off. They took the Monday of the week of Thanksgiving through Thanksgiving, returning that next Wednesday. Lesson plans were turned in Friday and they departed that Saturday morning.

What should we call them? The Fantastic Fool or the Silly Six? This happy group of travelers to Hungerville from Providence could well have been a traveling circus or a carnival tour. They never ceased talking and laughing. They ate. They drank. They joked, told jokes, and teased one another. Mordecai told about the time when he was in a wheelchair at Walter Reed Hospital when he and Fannie Mae made love when he yelled and told the nurses that he had gotten his finger caught in the wheel. They laughed so hard that Suzanne had to stop driving. She pulled over off the road so as to regain her composure.

They ate in restaurants, at rest stops for picnics, and McDonalds, Waffle Houses, and in the Jeep after stopping at places like Kentucky Fried Chickens and Wendy's drive throughs.

Patty Sue told about the fight between she and Fannie Mae in high school over Mordecai where she claimed to have come out the winner. Fannie refuted by saying, "Well, if you were the winner, how come you stopped flirting with my man?"

"Cause I didn't want to continue wallowing round on the ground showing my naked booty, cause I didn't wear no drawers and you didn't neither."

This sent everybody into a frenzy causing Mordecai to pull over. Ethyl Mae added, "The boys didn't have to try to look up your dresses. All they had to do was to look down and see everything "possible.""
This set off another laughing tremor and anytime anybody would mention the word "fight" the laughter would begin all over.

They arrived at home happy, healthy, and hilarious. The first stop was the Allison mansion. Tom and Peggy, with tears streaming from their eyes, kissed and embraced everyone. "Welcome home, baby. God has answered our prayers," said Peggy.

"Forgive me, Mommy and Daddy. I've been such a fool. Forgive me, Thelma Louise and Patty Sue. I'm sorry for the pain I've brought into your lives," Suzanne cried.

"You didn't hog whip and drag me along. I went on my own free will," said Patty Sue.

"Let's all go into the living room, kneel and pray," Peggy said. They did with all holding hands.

Peggy began: "Dear Lord, we thank You for giving our daughters back to us. We thank you for their health and sound minds once again. Thank You for the crew You assembled to carry out this dangerous mission—Mordecai, Fannie Mae, and Alonzo. Please continue to watch over us. Protect us and guide us. Amen."

As they departed, both Thomas and Peggy were embracing Suzanne simultaneously. Thelma Louise was hugging Patty Sue so hard she could hardly breathe, saying over and over again, "Thank you, Jesus, thank you, Jesus."

Mordecai, Fannie Mae, Mae Helen, and Ethyl Mae went home to their families. Reckon its possum eating time?

The next day about 10:00 a.m., Thomas Allison, Suzanne, and Peggy drove to Mordecai's spread. They got out and Thomas asked, "Y'all got any leftover possum to share?"

Both Suzanne and Rosa said, "Ugh."

'No, sir, Mr. Allison, all we got is pork chops, rice, and gravy. Care for some?"

"I was just playing with you. Naw, we are all full. Thelma Louise made us a great breakfast this morning of fried eggs, grits, biscuits, ham, sausage, bacon, syrup, hot coffee, and milk. We won't eat anymore until suppertime. Just came to talk and settle up."

As they sat around the kitchen table drinking lemonade, Thomas Allison said, "How much more money do I owe you?"

THE POSSUM HUNTER

"Nothing," said Fannie Mae. "We got a thousand twenty-five dollars and forty-three cents left over, and here it is."

As she attempted to hand it over, Thomas made the gesture of no by waving his hand "No need for "chunk change." Give it to your lovely daughter Rosa."

"Well, what about me?" asked Little Willie.

"Y'all can go on halfen," said Uncle Lonzo.

"Good idea," said Mordecai, "and thank you sir, Mr. Allison."

"Let's get away from this Mr. Allison and sir shit. From now on I'm Thomas and this is Peggy, and we don't need no sirs or ma'ams. OK?"

"OK," said Mordecai as he attempted to give him the keys to the Jeep. "Here's the keys to your new Jeep and there it is over there all cleaned up and shiny for you. Want me or Lonzo to drive it to your house?"

"Give the keys to Lonzo. He can drive it and keep it as his own. Here are the ownership papers, Lonzo. Sign here."

Alonzo jumped high off the ground and yelled, "Ooh wee, thank you, Lord! Thank you, Mr. Allison!"

"Now remember, I told you about that Mr. Allison stuff."

"All right, thank you, Thomas, for making me the first nigger in Hungerville to own a brand new Jeep and ain't nan nother one like it anywhere close around here." In the envelope with the papers was five thousand dollars cash and a plastic card allowing unlimited credit to the Allison's stores without payback.

"And now, Mordecai, for your courage, ingenious military mind and maneuvers, undertaking an impossible mission, risking your life to bring our daughters back to us and succeeding, I now present to you the deed to the sixteen acres on the lower forty along with the house in need of restoration. It is now yours."

Mordecai accepted, embraced Fannie Mae, shook hands with Thomas and embraced him also, fell to his knees, and cried like a baby. "Thank you, Lord, for making my dream come true. Now I know where I am going when I retire and we shall spend each summer and any vacation right here restoring the promised land." His whole family was overjoyed. Little Willie and Rosa both loved "back home—down South."

Along with the deed to the property, Mrs. Peggy Allison included ten thousand dollars cash to be used in helping to restore the land. Thomas Allison, Jr. placed a note promising unlimited free lumber from his sawmill to build or restore and there was a ten thousand dollar check from Rosemary, made out to a furniture company in High Point, North Carolina to begin furnishing their new home or summer cottage.

Fannie Mae and Mordecai felt that their mission was justifiable and that God was instrumental in directing them to undertake such an arduous task. They accepted these gifts as rewards from their deity. Suzanne sent nothing except this note:

Dear Mordecai, Fannie, and Alonzo,
Words alone cannot explain adequately the gratitude in my heart for you. I sincerely thank you for rescuing me and giving me back my life. I believe truly that you all are my guardian angels sent from Heaven above. Otherwise, why would you undertake such a formidable task, risking your own lives, plus the unborn baby's life? I shall not insult you by giving you material things or money. Your duty to me is priceless and cannot be measured or valued monetarily.

Instead, I offer you a lifetime of love, gratitude, and devotion. I shall be your humble servant whenever you need me. I will help in cleaning and restoring your house. I shall be your babysitter whenever you need me. You too, Alonzo, whenever you marry and have children. I shall help you decorate and bring in my interior decorator to assist if you so choose. Consider me your "Cleopatra Booker" of the South. When you get ready to go back up north, please call me so I can help you pack. And Alonzo, if you need me call and I'll come running, except in cleaning possums and coons.

I love you,
Suzanne

Thelma Louise and Patty Sue Garrison didn't have any money or material things to offer so they invited all of them over to a dinner at their shanty, soon to be a new house, as promised by Suzanne and agreed upon by her family.

As they all sat at the kitchen table to their meal of coon, fried chicken (for Rosa), potatoes, rice and gravy, black-eyed peas, collard greens, pork chops with cornbread and butter, Patty Sue slipped a note into the hand of Mordecai that he concealed in his pants pocket. They drank "sweet tea," buttermilk, lemonade, coffee, and Coca Colas. Patty Sue made sure that Mordecai got a Coke by placing one directly in his hand. They both remembered her giving him his first Coca Cola and smiled.

Rosa was happy with some of the best fried chicken that she had ever tasted and paid no attention to the others eating coon.

The dessert was served right along with the meal so there was no special time allocated for eating dessert. You ate your apple pie along with your rice pudding or blackberry cobbler anytime you wanted to. The homemade ice cream was sitting at the end of the table in a bucket of ice.

They were so full when they finished eating that most of them had to say "excuse me" for belching and secretly farting.

At the departure time, Thelma Louise hugged and kissed everyone, cried and said, "In the name of Jesus, thank you Mordecai, Fannie Mae, and Alonzo!"

Patty Sue, also with tears in her eyes, embraced them all and said, "I thank y'all from all of my heart and soul. God bless you!"

In his bathroom at home, Mordecai took the note handed him from Patty Sue from his pocket and read it. It read: "I hope you enjoyed the Coca Cola. I love and mean no disrespect to Fannie Mae, but anytime you want "some" you can get "some." I still love you. P.S.-G" (this stood for Patty Sue Garrison

Mordecai did not follow up on this offer but thought anytime in the future if he decided to stray, Patty Sue would be his "ace in the hole." He tore the note to pieces and flushed it down the commode.

* * * * *

Fannie and Mordecai went on back up to Rhode Island as the richest "colored folks" in, and from, Hungerville, Mississippi.

Mordecai would decide the future now. He was the man in control. No more Calvin Lucases, no more Fred Woullards, no more anybodies to deter him or consume his mind with thoughts that were not of his choosing or interest. He was 38 years of age now and his wife only 37. They had both invested some years in the Rhode Island teaching system. For full retirement benefits one would have to either reach the age of 55, or teach a total of twenty years. He now had 10 years at age 37 and Fannie Mae 7 years at age 36. If they taught three more years, then Fannie Mae would have taught 10 years at age 39 and he 13 years at age 40. They both could retire and receive one-half the benefits, which would come to about $1,500 a month each when they reached the age of 55 with his benefits coming one year before hers.

Their financial foundation was solid. They had over three hundred thousand dollars in their saving accounts, including stocks and bonds, in Rhode Island. They had the ten thousand dollars that Thomas Allison gave them deposited in First National Bank in Hattiesburg. They always had at least one thousand dollars cash stashed away at home for wining and dining or short weekend excursions and even an American Express card. He would have his disability check from the VA for life plus death benefits. If they sold their house in Providence, it should sell for at least three hundred thousand dollars. If they kept the house in Providence and rented it, they would have to charge the renters, whether they were Mae Helen and Ethyl Mae or anyone else, at least $1,800 a month. This would pay their house note plus give them four hundred dollars extra. To rent or lease such a house would require $1,800 down, $3,000 for a security deposit, and $1,800 for last month's rent, a total of $7,200 to begin with.

Most people would rather buy than lease but in a cosmopolitan area such as Providence, many people chose to lease or rent. People such as untenured professors, rich students, actors, actresses, professional athletes, or business personnel who had been transferred to the area by their companies or corporations who didn't wish to take permanent residence for fear of being transferred again.

THE POSSUM HUNTER

Mordecai and Fannie Mae would, of course, continue working when they returned to Mississippi. Any institute of learning in the state would highly welcome mathematician Ph.D. Fannie Mae Johnson. She would have no problem finding employment with decent pay. Mordecai, on the other hand, might not be so fortunate. His degrees from Tougaloo College and Mississippi State University should be assets to his successful teaching years in Providence, Rhode Island, and should also help boost his qualifications. He had passed, by the skin of his teeth, with Fannie Mae's tutoring, the National Teacher's Examination. This time they didn't cheat, but she tutored and taught him to pass after his third try.

First they would explore the possibilities of becoming members of the faculties of the University of Southern Mississippi or William Carey College, both located in Hattiesburg, Mississippi, and Jones Junior College, a few miles away in Ellisville, Mississippi. Each of these would be easy commuting distances from their new house "Glory Land." If they had to commute long distances, they might as well stay in Providence, they reasoned.

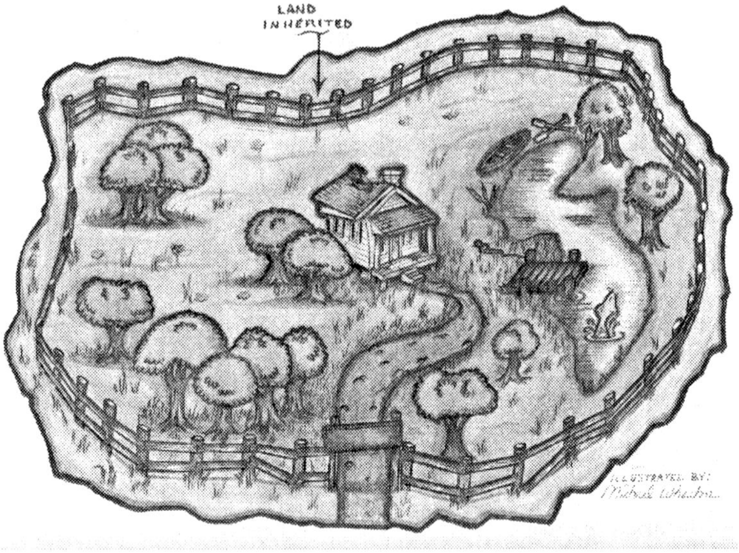
LAND
INHERITED
ILLUSTRATED BY:

Xanthus's Castle

The Building of Glory Land—Again

First, Mordecai had the land surveyed and fenced in. Then he hired his father Oscar along with Alonzo and his two brothers Jim and Johnnye B to work the land.

Their jobs would be to clean the land of weeds and unwanted shrubbery; cultivate and trim the fruit trees and berry bushes, plus the beautiful flowers; either hire a demolition team or themselves demolish the old mansion and take the pieces away. In its spot would be built a new house just like the one they lived in now in Providence. Mordecai obtained the original architectural blueprints, added some things and deleted some others, then hired a local contractor to build their dream castle. The contractor was required to use eight black men, including Oscar, Alonzo, Jim, and Johnnye B. The other four would be from Hungerville's vicinity poor folks. The building of the house would only cost one hundred fifty thousand dollars in Mississippi.

You see a one hundred thousand dollar house in Mississippi would be worth three hundred thousand dollars in Rhode Island and New England, period. Perhaps in New York and its surrounding areas such as Connecticut and New Jersey even more.

And so in the spring of 1983, Mordecai and Fannie Mae moved back to Hungerville, Mississippi. Along with them were their three children: baby Anthony, three years old and talking as though he were five; Rosa, "smart as a whip," who was twelve years old; and Little Willie, who was sixteen years old and had just completed his freshman year at Yale University with four A's and a B+ each semester. The one course that he could not master was philosophy. Who's gonna cry? He had already been accepted at Tougaloo where he decided to transfer to. It was his own decision to be more involved academically and socially involved with people of his own race. He knew that Tougaloo's academics could measure up with any school in America and, besides, he wanted to lose his virginity to a black female.

Their relocating was initiated by the University of Southern Mississippi offering Ph.D. Fannie M. Johnson an Associate Professor position with a beginning salary of $60,000. She would, of course, be required to teach during the summers her first two years with $5,000 extra. USM wanted Dr. Johnson so terribly they secured a job for her husband as Jones County's agricultural county agent, starting salary of $45,000, plus travel and a truck if he so desired.

Because Rosa asked for a little sister to play with, Mordecai and Fannie Mae, after two years, took a chance in their mature years and accommodated her with the birth of Gizzelle, named by Mrs. Booker who just happened to be there after she learned that Fannie Mae was pregnant again. They offered her a permanent place to stay for the winters if she so desired. "I'll give it some thought," she said.

Mrs. Booker and Fannie Mae gave to Mordecai a Japanese Yamaha four wheeler for Christmas so that he could negotiate the terrain's lower bottoms, inclines, bumps, and ditches close enough to get out and run or walk to where a possum or coon had been treed. Thus, he was again able to hunt again. Now, who would have thought that a Rhode Island woman would have the gumption to come up with an idea like this to resume Mordecai's passion? He could now hunt once more, using his ATV (all-terrain vehicle) Honda four tract. The other hunters could go on ahead and he would follow them on his "four wheeler," or lead them.

And so, my dear readers, I have taken you from a love story beginning with a raccoon hunt involving simple people with simple lives doing simple things, through the ethnology of different people with different characteristics, intermingling both, defining nothing that most of us do not encounter sometimes in our lives. We lust, we hunger, we suffer, we enjoy. Sometimes we are deceived. Sometimes we learn the

THE POSSUM HUNTER

truth that is often concealed inextricably from our minds but is revealed to us by someone of higher intellect. We love, we fight, we play, we rescue, and are rescued. We eat what we like regardless. We hunt, even if it is nothing more than a bargain at a store.

We all are victims of *in flagrante delicto*—the act of doing something wrong, especially like having illicit sex.

Happy hunting!

—S. Earl Wilson, III

And no, Thomas Wolfe, I disagree with your statement of "You cain't go home again."

Mordecai did!!

Or as the Mississippi author James Whorton, Jr. says: "Ending up where you started out."

As you all know, this is a story of fiction, but as in all my writings, truth is often disguised as fiction. There is always something educational to learn.

Three of the characters in this book are real live, authentic human beings. They are:

(1) Dr. Henry C. Foster, my college roommate, of Nashville, Tennessee who furnished my medical information and directed me how to find more. Here are some of his credentials:

Curriculum Vitae
Henry Wendell Foster, Jr., M.D.
CURRENT STATUS
Business Contact:Home Contact:
Meharry Medical College 4140 West Hamilton Road
Professor EmeritusNashville, TN 37218-1829
Department of Obstetrics and GynecologyHome 615-876-3781
1005 Todd BoulevardCell 615-337-5222
Nashville, TN 37208-3599Fax 615-299-0188
Business Telephone (615) 327-6284E-mail hwfoster@aol.com
Facsimile (601) 299-0188Social Security # upon request

CURRENT APPOINTMENTS
1998-PresentProfessor Emeritus, Obstetrics and Gynecology, Meharry Medical College
1975-PresentClinical Professor of Obstetrics and Gynecology, Vanderbilt University

OTHER ACTIVITIES
Jan 1995Nominated to become U.S. Surgeon General by President William Clinton
May 1995Recommended for confirmation for U.S. Surgeon General by the Senate Labor
Human Resources Committee

S. EARL WILSON, III

January 1996-December 2001 Senior Advisor to President Clinton on Teen Pregnancy Reduction and Youth Issues

PERSONAL DATA
Date and Place of Birth: September 8, 1933, Pine Bluff, Arkansas
Marriage: St. Clair Anderson, 1960-Present
Children: Myrna Faye, (Born 1962)
Henry Wendell, III (Born 1964)

EDUCATION
High School Diploma (Valedictorian), The Laboratory Schools, University of Arkansas at
Pine Bluff (formerly Arkansas AM&N College), Pine Bluff, Arkansas, 1950
B.S., Biology Major and Chemistry Minor, Morehouse College, Atlanta, Georgia, 1954
M.D., University of Arkansas School of Medicine, Little Rock, Arkansas, 1958

POST-GRADUATE TRAINING
Rotating Internship, Detroit Receiving Hospital, Wayne State University, Detroit, Michigan, 1958-1959
Captain, US Air Force Medical Officer, 1959-1961
General Surgery Residency, Malden Hospital, Malden, Massachusetts, 1961-1963
Obstetrics and Gynecology Residency, George W. Hubbard Hospital of Meharry Medical College, Nashville, Tennessee, 1963-1965

Henry W. Foster, Jr., M.D.Curriculum VitaePage 2

Senior Scholar-In-Residence, Association of Academic Health Centers, Washington, DC
(Sabbatical leave, 1994-1995

CERTIFICATION

Certified, American Board of Obstetrics and Gynecology, 1967
Recertified, American Board of Obstetrics and Gynecology, 1977
Recertified, American Board of Obstetrics and Gynecology, 1986

HONORARY DOCTORATE DEGREES

Doctor of Science, conferred by the University of Arkansas for the Medical Sciences, Little Rock, Arkansas, May 15, 1993

Doctor of Humane Letters, conferred by Emerson College, Boston, Massachusetts, May 12, 1996

Doctor of Science, conferred by Albany Medical College, New York, May 23, 1996

Doctor of Laws and Letters, conferred by the University of California, San Diego Medical School, San Diego, California, June 9, 1996

Doctor of Science, conferred by Northwestern University, Evanston Illinois, June 16, 2000

Doctor of Humane Letters, conferred by Hofstra University, Hempstead, New York, December
21, 2003

PAST MEHARRY APPOINTMENTS

Professor and Chairman, Department of Obstetrics and Gynecology, Meharry Medical College,
1973-1990

Chairman, Advisory Committee, Institutional Self-Study, Southern Association of Colleges and
Schools (SACS), 1973-1974

Chairman, Board of Directors, Meharry Medical Group, P.C. (Institution's medical practice plan), 1985-1988

Member, Appointment, Promotion and Tenure Committee, 1989-1990

Chairman, Institution's Annual Budget Committee, 1987-1988

(2) Mr. Donald P. Stone, my friend and fellow football teammate at Morehouse College, who really did forsake the field of chemistry to pursue civil rights endeavors. He is the author of the book *Fallen Prince*. Here are some of his credentials:

BIO SKETCH OF DONALD P. STONE

I was born in Opelika, Alabama, in 1935 to an AME minister and a school teacher. Aside from Opelika, I have lived in Dothan, Prattville, Prichard, Huntsville and Snow Hill. I presently live in Snow Hill, the home of my mother's people. I attended public schools in all of the aforementioned towns. However, I graduated from the famed **Snow Hill Institute**, the school founded by my grandfather, William James Edwards, in 1893. I attended Morehouse in 1953 becoming the third of ten descendants who have matriculated at Morehouse College. Among that ten is Spike Lee, the noted filmmaker and director. In high school, I ran track, played football, basketball, and baseball. I also sang in the choir and played alto saxophone in the band. I was valedictorian in a twenty-five member graduating class.

At Morehouse, I played varsity football and intramural track, basketball and softball. I was an All-City and All-Conference fullback for the "House." I majored in biology and minored in chemistry. Shortly after Morehouse, I became involved in the civil rights movement, and I was a member of the Student Non-Violent Coordinating Committee (SNCC), the African Liberation Support Committee, and the Black Workers Congress, all organizations attempting to make fundamental social and political change in the U.S. and Africa. In connection with these activities (opposition to the Vietnam War), I was sentenced to three and one-half years in federal prison and spent two years there.

The axis of my life has been political activism on the one hand and writing on the other. I have published one book and had two others destroyed by fire, including a biography of Booker T. Washington and several prison diaries and letters. I am presently preparing to publish a book of essays on politics and culture and am working on an autobiographical memoir.

THE POSSUM HUNTER

I am presently working to assist in the restoration of **Snow Hill Institute** and to develop a museum to honor the history of the school and its people.

(3) Howard Gleichenhaus. Here are his credentials.
Born November 18, 1943, Philadelphia, Pennsylvania.

Grew up in NYC (Bronx) literally in the shadows of Yankee Stadium and the Polo Grounds.

NYC public schools (K-11) and Spring Valley HS (grade 12).

BA, Biology, Southern Connecticut, 1965.
MA, Biology, Fairleigh Dickinson, 1968.
MA, Psychology, Fairleigh Dickinson, 1973.

S. EARL WILSON, III

Teacher:
St. Joseph's Regional High School, Montvale, 1968.
Clarkstown, 1969-2001, Jr. High North HS South HS Biology.
Taught Biology, Honors Biology, AP Biology, and some General Science.

Ran a photography business from 1974-1990 doing wedding portraits and Bar Mitzvahs with an occasional commercial job.

Married Fredda Kellman, 1973, also a Clarkstown teacher (Physical Education).
2 sons: Corey and Robert, now married. 1 grandchild on the way.

The boys are in business in Delray (Double Play Media, Inc.). They run ad campaigns for internet-based businesses.

Retired in 2001 and relocated to Delray Beach, FL, and now live in an "active adult" (over 55) community (Valencia Falls).

Started writing after retirement.

Edit a 30-page local monthly community paper, *The View from the Falls*, and write a monthly opinion column and a photography column.

Now back (small time) in a portrait business out of my home.

Since retiring I have taught myself Adobe Photoshop and consider myself good enough at it to be a professional photo retoucher and a fairly competent graphic artist. I do all community advertising for shows with large posters.

I have written nearly two dozen short stories (one contest win) as well as a completed novel called *Colquitt*. I now seek agent representation but, as you well know, getting published is hard.

THE POSSUM HUNTER

The story is set in the southern Georgia, county of Colquitt, specifically the city of Moultrie and the town of Doerun, in the late 1930's and is about murder and infidelity.

I have only one bit of advice for all retirees: Stay healthy and take care of yourself because this is definitely the best time of life!

From:Howard Gleichenhaus
Date:11/22/2007 9:16:25 a.m.
Subject: This made my Thanksgiving

I received this email from a student whom I had 7 years ago. Sometime you win the war.

Just wanted to keep you posted on my life...I'm graduating this May from Yale and have decided to work for McKinsey, a consulting firm in Manhattan. I've also applied to law schools (which I will hear back from in a month or two) and will be deferring for two years.

In other good news, I received Phi Beta Kappa this fall and will be attending the initiation ceremony in December. Thank you for recognizing my potential years before it came into full bloom. I hope all is well with you and your family and you have a very happy Thanksgiving!

Sincerely,
Marc Appel

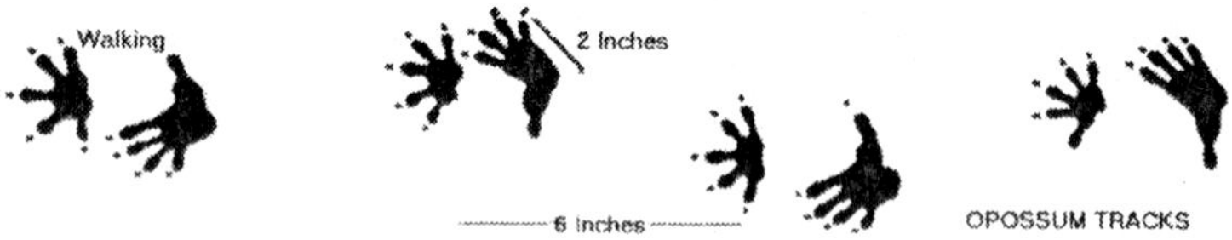
Walking
2 Inches
6 Inches
OPOSSUM TRACKS

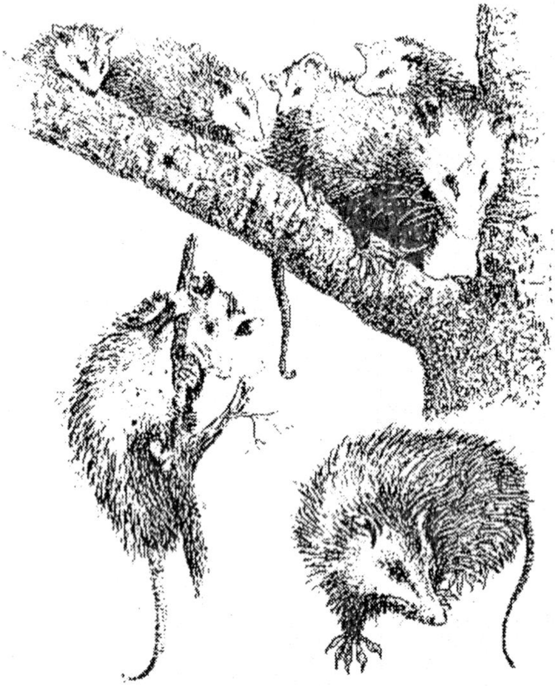

APPENDIX A

If after having read this enumeration and if like rainbows, you are inclined to pursue the profession of raccoon and/or opossum hunting, here are some things you should know.

OPOSSUM

The opossum is America's only marsupial. That is, it carries its young in its pouch. It is not a large rat and not even a rodent at all. It is more related to the Australian kangaroo. The opossum was named by the Algonquin Indian, *"pasum."* How we got the "o," nobody knows.

After the female opossum's honeymoon, she gives birth within 13 days to 12 or 13 babies. The babies are tiny (small enough that all of them could fit into a teaspoon), blind, naked, and helpless. The babies crawl into their mother's pouch where they latch on to a teat for nourishment. There they remain for three months. When they leave the pouch, they cling to their mother's fur for about 10 to 15 days. When they become too heavy to cling, one by one they drop off. This is the weaned stage and they are ready to forage for themselves. The mother is often referred to as "a four-legged bus."

The opossum lived during the age of dinosaurs and no doubt served as food for some of them.

It is not very good at fighting or defending itself and if attacked, it collapses and pretends to be dead (playing possum).

The average adult opossum is about the size of a housecat with shorter legs. It weighs from 6 to 15 pounds. Females are usually smaller than males. Both have 50 teeth, more than any land mammal.

S. EARL WILSON, III

The opossum has a narrow, tapered head with a spear-shaped muzzle, black eyes, a pink/reddish nose, bluish/black hairless ears, and a long, scaly tail. Its front and back feet have five white toes. The inner toe of each hind foot contains no claws and resembles a human's thumb. Its fur is grayish black except underneath, where it is creamy white with grayish tips.

The opossum's habitats range from wooded areas near streams, to farm fields, to patches of woods through forests and croplands. They seem to prefer places near permanent water areas.

The opossum is a very clean animal and some people say, "It tastes like chicken!"

left front

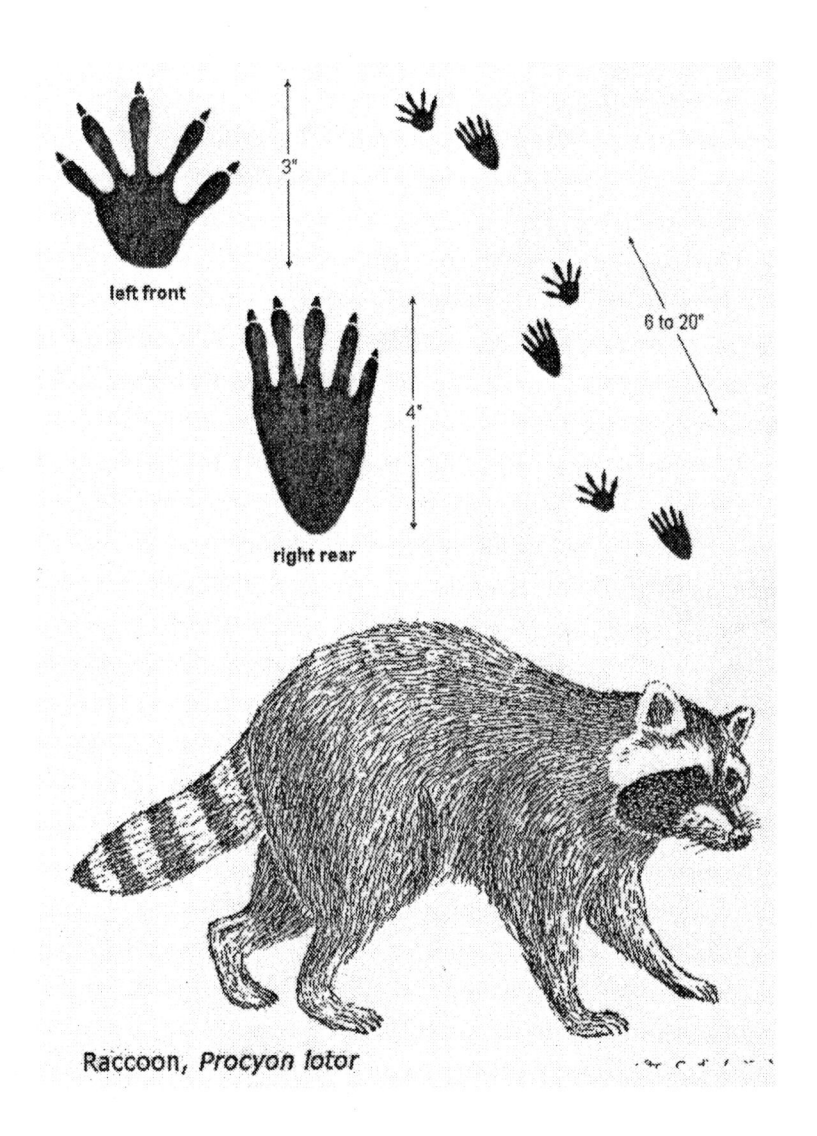

3"

right rear

4"

6 to 20"

Raccoon, *Procyon lotor*

THE RACCOON

The raccoon is easily recognized by its striped masked face and bushy ringed tail. Its fur is from 1-2 inches long, is grizzled gray or sometimes black with silver tips, but can range from light brown to dark black. It has a broad head, pointed nose, black eyes and ears that are about one and one-half inches long that stand straight up.

It has invaded almost every habitat and is found even in towns and cities. Its success is due to its ability to lie in a variety of habitats and survive on different kinds of food. Normally, the raccoon feeds along waterways, streams and lakes. It is a swimming hunter, seeking fish, frogs, turtles, turtle eggs, and crayfish. It will also capture mice and muskrats along the banks of waterways. On lands it searches for insects, nuts, berries, fruits, young birds, and bird eggs.

In certain arrears the raccoon is considered a nuisance because it raids poultry and wild fowl breeding sites. It also feasts on the farmer's corn and other crops. Because of its thumb it can use its hand very well while scavenging for food, such as turning knobs and overturning trash/garbage cans.

Raccoons have been trapped and hunted for their fur since early America. "Coonskins" were once used as headwear and as currency. Because of this the raccoon has been introduced into other countries like Europe and Russia.

The female gestation period is 60-73 days and she gives birth to 3 to 4 babies. The female will mate with only one male a season, avoiding all others while the male raccoon will mate with different females.

These nocturnal animals differ depending on their species but in general, their length, including the tail, ranges from 20-40 inches and their weight between 10-35 pounds. Males are generally larger than females. A baby raccoon is called a "kit."

The raccoon is a clean animal that often washes its food before it eats. As some people say, "It tastes like lamb."

Happy Hunting!
S. Earl Wilson, III